THE NURSING HOME HOAX

THE NURSING HOME HOAX

by

Shelley Thrasher & Ann Faulkner

2025

THE NURSING HOME HOAX

ISBN 13: 978-1-63679-806-6

This Trade Paperback Original Is Published By
Bold Strokes Books, Inc.
P.O. Box 249
Valley Falls, NY 12185

First Edition: July 2025

Credits
Editor: Jenny Harmon
Production Design: Stacia Seaman
Cover Design by Inkspiral Design

Acknowledgments

The village that supported the writing of our first collaboration/first novel/first cozy mystery is vast. Neighbors and family who made space for us to write instead of expecting us to perform our usual roles include Tami, Susan, Marion, all the many Browns and Thrashers, and Rebel and Darryl. Friends asked about our progress and applauded even the most microscopic advances, including Pat, Susan, DebiSu, Carol, Ouida and John, Carolyn and Jim, Sarah, April, Pud, Barbara, and Linda and the members of both the Monday and Wednesday writing groups, Ad-lib, Sew Much Fun, and Tea at Troy's. We interviewed a number of people whose experiences were similar to those of characters in our story, among them Barbara, Sandy, Caroline, Christie, Therese, Beverly, Arleta, Brook and Lennon, and Keyri. They added accuracy and depth to the characters we created. At Bold Strokes Books, we were sustained by Rad, Sandy, and Cindy and saved from innumerable muddles by our diligent editor, Jenny. THANK YOU ALL!

To the seniors in our lives,
too many of whom have already left us behind.
Thank you for all you've given us.
Bill Faulkner
Cheryl Gregory
John Harwood
Ned Morris
Dana Stahl
Josephine Thrasher

CHAPTER I

An Old Friend Returns

Ping.

> *Can we talk, Marilee? I have news about Edith.*
> *Sure, Taylor. What's up?*
> *She's in Texas!*
> *Really? She's been gone, what, sixty years?*
> *Yeah. Never thought we'd see her again.*
> *But why's she here after so long?*

Taylor called out, "Lois. Will you bring me that old photo album, the one with the brown leather cover?"

Her executive assistant immediately brought it in. Lois—the granddaughter of a now-retired Black housekeeper—knew where everything was. She'd been with Taylor since high school, living in the garage apartment out back while working and attending college part-time. Taylor winced as she realized once again that Lois was about to finish her social work degree and would be moving on soon.

Riffling through it to a group of photos from the early 1960s, she found her favorite. There they stood, stairsteps—Marilee, tall, athletic, dark-haired; in the middle, Edith, average height, sturdy, her hair in a medium-length Afro; and Taylor, short, petite, and blond. Three native-Texan coeds.

Her phone pinged with another text. *Where'd you go?*

Taylor fondly recalled that day—the three of them, arms around each other's waists, standing in front of the famous tower at the University of Texas at Austin.

Just reminiscing.

You can do that later. Is something wrong with Edith? Or did she just finally decide she wants to live in the Lone Star State again?

Okay. Okay. Hold on a minute. Taylor closed the album. *Edith has a good reason to come back.*

What? Finally homesick?

She broke her hip.

Oh, no. How bad?

Evidently bad enough for her to come to her senses and fly home. Why don't you call me?

I thought you'd never ask. You know I'd rather talk than type any day.

But texting's quicker. Taylor glanced at her smartwatch.

For you, maybe. You're a busy lawyer. But I'd like it even better if we could discuss this situation over lunch. Hint. Hint.

Taylor grinned. Eating out was one of Marilee's favorite pastimes. She looked at her empty reception area, Lois the only one there. Was she getting pickier about accepting clients, or did more people prefer younger representation these days? Maybe she should try something new, something she and Marilee could do together. She sighed and typed a quick message. *You're right. I'm hungry anyway. Meet you at Chat n Chew in five? How far away are you?*

I'm at Half Price Books. So not far. See you soon.

❖

Taylor glanced around the country-cooking restaurant located on New Eden's town square. Her ancestors had moved here to the heart of East Texas before the Civil War, and at times the area didn't appear to have changed all that much.

She walked over to a quiet table in the corner and sat there until Marilee finally poked her head through the front door and waved. Taylor waved back. "Right on time, as usual," she said sarcastically, glancing at her watch again. *Five minutes late.*

"Of course. It usually doesn't take too long to get anywhere in New Eden, but we do have some traffic today. And I had to wait in line to pay for my new books." Marilee sat in one of the well-padded chairs that encouraged lunch patrons to linger. "You know, I've begun to realize that I'm bored. I know you'll never retire, but why don't we come up with something we can do together? Wouldn't that be fun?"

Taylor picked up a plastic-coated menu, though she had it memorized. "I just had the same thing on my mind. How about becoming private eyes? We could right all the wrongs here in New Eden." She chuckled.

Marilee glowed. "Wow. Do you mean it? I can't imagine anything I'd like better. We could use Bradford's Arbor as our headquarters. What can we call ourselves?"

Taylor stared at her. "I was just kidding."

"But I'm not. We could ask Lois to help us, until she gets a full-time job in social work. I'm sure this town has a lot of wrongs for us to right. We could call ourselves Senior Sleuths and focus on the older people here. That's a group we both can identify with. We could make a real contribution."

"Are you serious?" Taylor asked. "It *would* be fun to chase wrongdoers and do good deeds for people whose needs are often overlooked. In fact, I just read an article in the *Dallas Morning News* about AI-assisted cybercrimes and how they've affected senior citizens."

Marilee was almost jumping up and down in her chair. "We could be like Nancy Drew and her sidekicks, except with a lot more experience and know-how. How fun!"

Having Marilee come to live with her had certainly brightened Taylor's life. But just now, they had other things to take care of—mainly food. "I'm hungry, Marilee. And I can't wait to tell you more about Edith."

Marilee brightened even more when their waitress arrived.

Taylor held up three fingers to the woman, who nodded and set down a glass of ice water.

And after Marilee held up one finger, the waitress gave her a huge glass of iced tea, which Marilee sipped immediately. "Thanks," she said. "It's already hot outside, and it's just May."

"Sure is," the woman said as she disappeared into the kitchen.

Taylor slid the irrelevant menu back between the plastic napkin holder and the bottle of tabasco on their table. Then she waved at the four well-dressed ladies sitting at a square table in the far corner, who looked up from their mah-jongg tiles for a second. She'd learned to play and found the game challenging, though it certainly could take up a lot of time she never had enough of. Also, she'd always managed to do some gardening, sing in the local Methodist Church choir, serve on several boards, plus play tennis. But her lawyering activities had always come first.

"If it hadn't been for Edith and the civil rights movement, we might have led lives more similar to many of those women's," Taylor said, tilting her head toward them. "As an African American active in civil rights, Edith helped us engage with the world in a new way, didn't she?"

Taylor gazed around the room at the other, mostly elderly, customers leisurely eating lunch. She'd known some of them since she was a kid, but what were their lives like now? Did they need two little old ladies to help them solve whatever problems life handed them?

"Becoming friends with Edith definitely changed our lives," Marilee said. "Maybe, when she feels better, she'd like to join our team of detectives. She could even move into Bradford's Arbor with us."

Taylor took a deep breath, enjoying Marilee's excitement. "I certainly agree about Edith. Do you know much about broken hips?"

"Not exactly. But after having both knees replaced several years ago, I could write a book about mobility impairment. What have you learned about Edith's condition?"

"Not much. She's had hip replacement surgery, but I'm not sure what kind of shape she's in now." Taylor checked her watch. "The service is kinda slow today, isn't it?"

"Like I always tell you, this is Chat n Chew, Taylor. This is the part where we chat about Edith. Eating can wait a while, though I am hungry."

Taylor blew out a long breath. "A Dallas hospital social worker called me out of the blue earlier and said Edith was initially treated for her broken hip in Ghana. And then she asked to be transferred to a hospital in Texas."

Marilee unwrapped the cellophane from a couple of crackers. "I wonder why."

"Maybe she *did* finally get homesick. Or wanted a change of scenery. But more than likely she feels like she's done all she can in Africa and wants to spend some time where she grew up."

"Will we get to see her much? Texas is a pretty big state." Marilee poured three packets of sugar into her iced tea.

"We have a very good chance."

"What do you mean?"

"The food's really taking its own sweet time to get here today, isn't it?"

Marilee stared at her suspiciously. "What are you not telling me about Edith? Are you avoiding something?"

"Well, according to the social worker, she flew to Dallas for hip replacement surgery." Taylor teased a saltine from its cellophane wrapping.

"Great. We can go visit her."

"We certainly can. And that's not all." Taylor bit into the cracker. "The social worker said that after Edith had recovered enough to leave the hospital, she had to spend some time recuperating in a rehab center. That's why our names came up."

"So where's the rehab facility? Can't we visit her there?"

Taylor put her half-eaten cracker on her napkin. "That's what I've been dying to tell you. We can see her this afternoon. She's in rehab right here in New Eden."

"That's great. Which nursing home is she in?" Marilee scooted forward in her chair.

"Silverado. You know, the nice one just past the local junior high school."

Marilee clapped three times, then held up her left hand in a Hook 'em Horns sign. "How great. That's only a mile or so from the house. And here come your steak salad and my meatloaf, mashed potatoes, and green beans. Plus, my piece of apple pie they always include." She unwrapped her silverware. "I can't wait to see Edith. Can you? The three of us working to protest segregation in Austin is among my most cherished memories."

CHAPTER II

Visiting Silverado

Taylor's smirk made Marilee want to poke her, but at least she didn't have to roar around town in Taylor's little blue hornet of a car.

"Let's go," Taylor said with her usual impatience.

Marilee mumbled as she chewed her meatloaf. "Hold on to your hat! I want to swallow my lunch first. I don't know how you can wolf down a salad so fast."

As the two of them settled into Marilee's five-year-old Nissan Rogue, Taylor grumbling about having to ride in such an old wreck, Marilee prompted Taylor to pick up the story of Edith's reappearance in their lives that she'd started during lunch.

"Edith and I haven't been in touch very much in the last few years, though I know a few basic facts about her life," Taylor said as Marilee backed out onto one of the four main streets of New Eden and headed south. "Her husband died of cancer about five years ago, and the three kids had been gone for quite a while by then. The older two are both married and practicing medicine in England. And the youngest became an architect in the Netherlands." Taylor twisted around to stare out the back window of Marilee's car.

"What's the matter? Did I run over something in the road?"

"No. I just wanted to see how many cars are backed up behind us. I feel like we're leading a funeral procession."

"At least we're not stretched out in the rear end of an ambulance heading toward the hospital."

"Ha, ha. I'll have you know I've never been in a major wreck."

"But how about all those fender-benders and speeding tickets you save up every month and then get one of your judge pals to excuse?"

"Okay. Okay. Let's don't get personal." Taylor stopped fidgeting quite so much.

"You were saying...about Edith? What about her life in Africa after her kids left?" Marilee asked.

"All right. Evidently, she just disappeared into her work. The clinic she and her husband had opened became her entire life. The social worker who called me somehow gathered a lot of personal info. She told me Edith slept on a cot in her office a lot of nights, and only when her staff insisted would she go home for a bath and a nap."

"How did the social worker find out all that?" Marilee asked, slowing down at the next intersection. She could probably have made it through the yellow light that was just about to turn red, but why push it?

"Oh, for heaven's sakes, Marilee. We could already be hearing this story from Edith if you'd let me drive."

Marilee pushed her glasses up on her nose as she began to poke along even more now. She didn't know what got into her at times, but it amused her to watch Taylor try to dial back her impatience.

"Actually, one of Edith's colleagues emailed me last year about her concerns," Taylor finally said, at last focusing more on her story than on the road. "I tried to reach out to Edith, but she was distantly polite. She obviously wanted to tell me to mind my own business."

Marilee turned right at the intersection after the light changed and thought she heard Taylor gritting her teeth. "Edith was always independent. But we had a pretty close relationship."

"You're probably right, but she's acted so distant in the last few years I almost quit trying to keep up with her. She obviously broke her hip during that silent spell. I'm surprised to learn she's nearby and wants to see us."

Taylor finally settled back into her seat as they neared the local junior high school.

Marilee inched past the long brick building that fronted the street, doing fifteen miles an hour, though the signs clearly stated the speed limit was twenty. She didn't see any students outside, but you never knew when one might pop up. Then, finally, she said, "That's totally different from the Edith we knew in college. Remember how good she was at making friends?" Marilee spotted a dog trying to cross the road and hoped it didn't dart out in front of her. "In spite of the tension around integration, Edith was always the first one to invite us to dinner at her residence hall. What was its name?"

"The Almetris Co-op," Taylor said immediately. "Can you believe that was the only place on campus for Black coeds to live? Not that we had that many African American students at UT back in the sixties."

Marilee slowed and clicked on her blinker. "Yes. And I recall what interesting times we had at the Y. Remember how we protested against all the segregated facilities on campus and at the businesses up and down the Drag? When we were freshmen, not even the movie theaters on that main street through campus were integrated. That's almost unbelievable now," Marilee said. "But I'll never get over the impact Edith had on you. She was so devoted to medicine and committed to her family's dream of having one of their own return to Africa to serve people. You two had a lot in common."

"In what way?" Taylor asked.

"You both lived out your family's dream instead of your own, though I'm not sure what Edith really wanted to do with her life."

"I know, dear one," Taylor said gently. "Obviously both Edith and I did what our families expected rather than what we wanted. But overall she and I have lived useful, fulfilling lives. As have you, evidently."

Marilee had barely pulled into a parking place near the front door, when Taylor had her hand on the door handle, threatening to open it before the Rogue stopped. "Well, we're here," she said. "And I can't wait to catch up with Edith. Let's go!"

❖

Marilee and Taylor hurried into the foyer of the Silverado Nursing Home, a city-owned facility familiar to Taylor. She had talked about visiting older friends here most of her adult life, especially her father. Marilee hadn't been inside before, but the large building appeared clean and well kept.

"Hi," Taylor said to the receptionist, who was sitting in a cubbyhole to their left. "We're here to visit Dr. Eyidah. Is she around?"

"Do you mean Dr. Edith? She was just here a minute ago. Why don't you try her room? Number 108. I'll let her know you're on the way."

They walked past a wall covered with framed photos of men in uniform to their left and found the room easily. Soon, Taylor was rapping on the door. "Open up, Edith. Your two favorite Longhorns are here!"

Edith softly replied, "Do come in. The door's not locked." As they entered, Edith struggled to stand up from her wheelchair but sat back down when Marilee and Taylor urged her to stay put. Gesturing for them to sit, she studied them. After all, they hadn't seen each other for sixty years. Her eyes filled with tears. "I never thought I'd be around you two again. I've really missed you."

"We've missed you, too, and I'm sorry I didn't write more often," Marilee said as she sat on a chair near Edith. "But I never forgot you and our great time together at UT."

Edith picked up a Kleenex and wiped her eyes. "I didn't forget you two either, but I was so busy—first working, and then working and raising a family. And after that, as the children grew up and moved away and my husband became ill, my practice began to take up even more time. After he died, the only thing I did was work."

Grasping the arm of the wheelchair, Edith ran her fingers gently along its padded surface. "So many people needed me, and I was good at helping the really sick ones. After a while, somehow that became all I could do." Edith slumped in her chair, not looking at either of them, shredding the Kleenex she still held.

"I figured you were working too hard and ignoring your own health," Taylor said sympathetically, standing up and walking toward the room's only window. "But how in the world did you break your hip?"

"I slipped and fell. It's as simple as that. Old bones don't respond to falls as well as young ones do. I got patched up in Kumasi but suddenly I realized I'd probably done all the good I could over there. And for the first time, I felt homesick for Texas."

"Well, it was about time," Marilee said, trying to make Edith loosen up.

And Edith did chuckle a bit. "After I felt well enough to travel, my assistant flew with me to Dallas, where she helped me settle in a nice orthopedic hospital, but she couldn't stay, so I was there all by myself, not moving around much after surgery." She paused. "But at least I was back in Texas."

"Why didn't you let us know?" Marilee asked. "We would have been up there in a flash."

"I believe you. But I had no idea where you were, Marilee. All I had was Taylor's contact information."

Taylor asked gently, "And why didn't you use it?"

Edith gazed at them long and hard. "Not everybody would

welcome a call from somebody they hadn't seen in sixty years, now would they?"

Marilee put her arm around Edith and squeezed. "But we aren't *everybody*, now are we?"

Edith slowly shook her head. "No."

Marilee smiled gently, her heart beating faster as so many memories from their college days rushed through her. "I'm so sorry I didn't write and let you know about my husband's death," she said, "and about bumping into Taylor by accident several months ago. I've been so caught up in my own life I've become a hermit of sorts. A little bored, in fact, though Taylor and I were just discussing a good way to remedy that situation."

"It's quite all right," Edith said. "I suppose, at our age, we all have a lot of major changes to deal with, and not as much energy to deal with them as we used to have. But how did you and Taylor get together again, and what kind of remedy are you two considering?"

Marilee and Taylor glanced at each other. "We do have a story to tell and would love to let you know about the exciting new venture we're contemplating," Marilee said. "But first, I'd like to hear a little more about your situation, Edith."

"What's it like for you to be back here in East Texas after this long?" Taylor asked.

"The staff are kind, and the food reminds me of Grandmom's house, God rest her soul." She took a long breath, but then her expression changed, and her dark eyes flashed. "And I'm finally well enough to get out of this room and meet more of the residents. In fact, I just heard about something, a scam I think, that's going on here that has several folks upset."

"Tell us more," Taylor said. "This is really a coincidence. Marilee and I were just discussing that we should team up as detectives to help elders who've been victimized. I fancy myself as a mature Nancy Drew, and Marilee fits the bill as one of her sidekicks. We even have a name for ourselves—Senior Sleuths. Maybe we could find our first case here. What's your opinion?"

Edith's eyes twinkled. "You two haven't changed a bit since college. Always wanting to right wrongs wherever you find them. And I suspect plenty of the people out here would appreciate your services. In fact, maybe I could be part of your team."

"Well, let us get our new venture up and running, not to mention getting you fully rehabbed, and then maybe we'll be ready for a new partner," Taylor said, her eyes sparkling, her tone mischievous. "But first, perhaps you can tell us what's going on out here."

"You know we'll do whatever we can to help," Marilee said.

Edith gave a smile, at once warm and reserved, making Marilee recall how, as a teenager in Austin, with her serious demeanor, Edith had always commanded respect.

"In our beauty salon the other day," Edith said, "I heard some of the women talking about a fellow resident who got a call from a young relative asking for money immediately to avoid jail."

"By the way, your hair does look nice," Marilee said.

"Thank you, though I bet you never thought you'd see all this gray in it." Edith patted the back of her head. "But to get back to my story, whoever called sounded like the woman's grandson. He said he was in trouble and needed money. But he's on a trip in Costa Rica, out of cell phone range, so she knew the call was a fake." Edith shook her head as if she was getting tired. "Just then, though, another woman, who was waiting for a shampoo, overheard the story and started crying."

Marilee paid closer attention to Edith. Maybe something bad actually was going on out here. Edith had always been observant and insightful. "Why was she crying?"

"The poor thing admitted that the same thing happened to her, but she paid the money! I felt so sorry for her. Now she's concerned about how she'll be able to afford to stay here. I don't know what she'll do." Edith clenched her fists, her face clouded. "The police were contacted but didn't seem interested in helping."

"What you're describing sounds like the AI-assisted phone scams I've been reading about lately," Taylor said.

"How does something like that work?" Marilee and Edith asked at the same time.

"Well, it's not that big a mystery." Taylor adopted her lawyer voice. "Scammers can use a short audio clip of someone's voice."

"But where would they get a clip like that?" Marilee asked.

"Most likely from the message on your cell phone. If you've ever posted anything that shows you talking, you're fair game. All a crook needs to create a fake message from an audio clip is a cheap voice-cloning program, and he's in business. I even read about something named PrankGPT that lets users make prank phone calls using an AI-powered voice."

Marilee shook her head. "What's this world coming to?"

"Well, at least some of us want to help innocent people fight such schemes," Taylor said, her eyes gleaming. "This is right up our alley!"

Chapter III

AI Hoaxes

Taylor's new next-door neighbor waved from her front porch as Taylor pulled into her driveway. "Hi there. Nice weather we're having."

Taylor looked toward her own house just in time to see Marilee wave, then disappear inside. "It sure is," she said. "We better enjoy it before it turns as hot as blazes. Welcome back. How was your trip?"

"Oh. Fantastic. France in the springtime is so romantic, even if I was traveling with my friend instead of my late husband, God rest his soul."

Though this woman and her husband had moved into the house next door about eighteen months ago, she and Taylor had spent very little time getting to know one another. Taylor had offered the usual condolences and casseroles after the husband's death, but beyond that she hadn't had any significant contact with Barb. At least she'd remembered her name. After Marilee had moved in that spring, they'd only had the briefest of introductions until Barb asked if they'd take care of her house plants while she and her younger friend took a two-week river cruise through France.

"You'll have to tell me all about it sometime," Taylor said, just as Marilee emerged back out through the side door of the house. "France is one of my favorite places."

"Hello, there," Marilee said. "Has Taylor been confiding in you about our latest brainstorm?"

"Well, no," Taylor said. "In fact, I was just saying—"

Marilee hurried toward them. "Hi, Barb. Taylor and I have been talking about making a major change in our lives. Do you have a minute?"

Barb jerked her head toward Marilee, possibly startled that her trip of a lifetime to France had been eclipsed so abruptly, but she shrugged good-naturedly. "Well, why don't you two come up here on the porch and catch me up on this major change you're contemplating?" She pointed to the striped chaise lounge nearby and sat in the armchair next to it.

After Marilee was seated beside Taylor, she immediately said, "Well, as you've probably noticed, Taylor and I have finally settled into our new living arrangement." She waved toward Taylor's large home. "With all that done, we're both beginning to feel a little underemployed. Taylor's practice is tapering off, and I have my volunteer work, but we could do more for the community and with ourselves."

Barb nodded, as if wanting to know more.

"So *more* has happened," Taylor said. "As luck would have it, our best friend from college, Edith, recently turned up here in town."

"Well, how nice. I'm glad to hear that," Barb said.

Marilee reclaimed the storytelling. "She's recovering from a broken hip that happened when she was practicing medicine in West Africa."

"You don't say."

"But that's not the most interesting part of the story, Barb. Edith has discovered that someone is using AI to steal money from several of her fellow residents at Silverado." Marilee paused to take a breath. "The police apparently aren't doing much about it, so Taylor and I have decided to become amateur sleuths like Nancy Drew and investigate the situation. Try to see what we can find out."

"I certainly remember all those Nancy Drew books I read when I was a girl, but what's AI?" Barb asked, frowning.

The front screen door opened, and a middle-aged woman popped out, carrying a tray of iced teas. "It's artificial intelligence, dear," she proclaimed to Barb. "It has to do with computers constructing information, such as reports, pictures, and even voices. Would anyone like a glass of tea?"

"Tea, yes. Computers?" Barb shrugged. "Well, count me out if it has to do with computers. I've never had any use for them and don't plan to start now. But do let me introduce my friend, traveling companion, and tea bringer, Shannon Hoyt. Shannon and I met at the local quilt show last year, and we have been friends ever since."

Marilee said, "Wow! Have I just discovered new soul mates? I love sewing, too. In fact, I volunteer in the costume shop for the Texas Shakespeare Festival in Kilgore every year."

The fiftysomething friend raised an eyebrow at Taylor. "I heard part of your conversation. Wouldn't dealing with cyber criminals be risky? It sounds like you could be flirting with danger."

Clearly bubbling with excitement, Marilee turned to her. "We don't know much about it yet, but from what I understand, some crooks are using AI to intimidate their victims. For instance, they might call you sounding exactly like one of your young relatives being held for ransom. 'If you don't pay up, they'll hurt me,' they usually say."

"Well, I never—" Barb said. "What's this world coming to?"

"But some people are beginning to learn how to fight back," Taylor said. "In the case we just heard about, the elderly woman who received the call simply hung up because she knew her grandson was out of the country and unable to use his cell phone."

"I read about that type of scam recently," Shannon said. "I guess the technology is developing so rapidly, it's getting easier for con men to be convincing. A company in Hong Kong lost millions when the senior staff transferred all their shares in response to fake AI-generated instructions from something that sounded exactly like their boss."

"You're right," Marilee said.

"We don't know a lot about what's going on," Taylor said, "That's why we've decided to try to help people, especially older ones like us and the residents at Silverado, avoid any more hoaxes like this. Many of the people out there are living on a fixed income and don't have anywhere to turn if someone swindles them out of their life savings." She glanced at each of them. "How does that sound as a new career for octogenarians like us?" Taylor beamed. "And we even have a name for this new venture."

"How exciting. What is it?" Barb asked.

"We've decided to call ourselves the Senior Sleuths," Taylor said. "We'll be a grown-up Nancy Drew and her friends, committed to righting the wrongs affecting elders in this fast-paced world."

Marilee chimed in. "Taylor and I won't be physically combatting criminals, of course, but we believe our years of experience will help us uncover and thwart extortion schemes and other scams. How does that sound?"

"I like it," Shannon said. "What a good idea. Will you try to work with the police? Or on your own, like Nancy Drew did most of the time?"

Taylor and Marilee stared at each other. "We truly haven't discussed all the details yet," Taylor said, "but I suppose if we get into a potentially dangerous situation, it would be nice to have a little support from the professionals."

"In fact," Marilee said, "right after we left Silverado, I suggested to Taylor that maybe we could go visit the chief of police, let him in on our plans, and ask his opinion about what's going on at Silverado. We know the police were called and didn't seem very interested, but maybe if we can give them a little more information, they'll want to be involved."

Shannon frowned. "Good luck with that. I know the New Eden Chief of Police, too. We were in high school together in Oak Cliff, and he was known as an ignorant, know-it-all bully. I'm not being very charitable, but I'd advise you two to steer clear of him. We bumped into each other recently in town, and he hasn't changed a bit."

Taylor tightened her lips, trying to force herself not to shake her head. She and Shannon were definitely on the same wavelength.

"It must be obvious I don't have a very high opinion of the police chief, Taylor. Isn't there someone else you could talk to?" Shannon asked.

Marilee spoke up. "You just met Taylor, so you wouldn't know she'd truly enjoy blasting into the station making accusations, leveling complaints, and getting us stonewalled from the get-go. As I say that out loud, I wonder if talking with the chief is a bad plan."

"I certainly think so," Shannon said. Her face had lost its color, and she looked as if she might faint.

Taylor moved to her side and spoke quietly to Shannon. "Sit down for a minute, won't you. I know the police chief slightly, having met him in court several times, and I share your opinion that he's a jerk. But I think we should make an effort to let the police know what's going on."

Shannon looked at Taylor gratefully. "As long as you know what he's like, and maybe take Marilee with you as a witness."

Marilee said, "I could even take the lead and keep the conversation from getting confrontational."

Shannon took another sip of her tea, color gradually returning to her cheeks. "I wish you two good luck. But please don't mention my name. That could bring on a major conflict."

"Sounds like a plan to me," Marilee said.

"Well, good luck with your new venture," Barb said, moving

to Shannon's side. "I think I better get this one inside out of the heat. She looks a little peaked."

"I'd really like to hear all about your cruise through France," Taylor said, standing and then helping Marilee up from the chaise lounge. "I bet you two saw some fabulous sights."

Barb wrapped her arm around Shannon. "We did, and I'll be forever grateful to this one here for treating me to such an amazing, expensive trip. We have some pictures we'd love to share with you. If you have any spare time from your sleuthing."

❖

On their way back across the yard to their front door, Taylor remained silent. "Are you thinking what I'm thinking?" Marilee asked.

"Probably. Do you believe this 'good friend' Shannon is on the level? She's certainly likeable, and we share the opinion that our police chief is a joke, but she definitely didn't want us talking to him or using her name. Could they have had legal clashes? And that makes me wonder where she got the money to pay for that kind of trip she and Barb took. Barb worried a lot about finances after her husband died and left her unexpected debts."

"Good point. Shannon was supportive of the Senior Sleuths' idea, and she and Barb both love sewing. But when we mentioned talking with the police chief, she was really vehement about avoiding him. What's that about? A guilty conscience? Could she possibly be involved in these scams? Like you, I thought we'd found a kindred soul, but she seemed about to pass out when we talked about meeting with him," Marilee said.

"While it's on my mind," she said as they climbed their front steps, "let me apologize if I made you sound like a relentless tornado, Taylor. You obviously can summon tact when you want to, and I actually would like to go see the chief and have you along with me to talk to him. I want to learn about this sleuthing business along with you, and this could be a perfect first lesson.

If I make an appointment for tomorrow morning, are you free to come, too?"

"Sure! I wouldn't miss this meeting for the world." Taylor held the door for Marilee and gave her a quick peck on the cheek as she passed.

CHAPTER IV

Speaking to the Chief

The next morning, Taylor threw on her robe and then gave Marilee a big hug when they bumped into each other out in the hall. "We've got to get moving," she said, kissing Marilee's soft cheek. "Our appointment at the police station is at nine thirty. What do you want for breakfast?"

"I'll fix us some yogurt and muesli while you hop in the shower," Marilee said. "I'm not taking a chance on ptomaine from your cooking this morning. This meeting is too important. I'll see you in the kitchen in twenty minutes."

When a still-damp Taylor entered the kitchen fifteen minutes later, breakfast was sitting on the table in a pool of morning sunlight. The cheerful kitchen had been repainted a warm yellow only a few months earlier, and now the room welcomed their planning session.

"I can't wait to find out what our cretinous chief of police has to say about these terrible crimes at Edith's nursing home and why New Eden's finest haven't lifted a finger to investigate," Taylor said. "Do we have any blueberries? This muesli is a little dry."

"We actually do have some fresh blueberries I bought at the Piggly Wiggly yesterday." As Marilee set a bowl of berries on the table, she added, "Let's strategize a minute. You just called the chief a cretin. Is that any way to start a conversation? I know you might not say the word to his face, but even thinking it could tilt the discussion downhill."

"Of course I wouldn't say *cretin* to that cretin's face. Even though he's probably aware of my opinion of his police work from the times I've cross-examined him in court. But what are you getting at?"

"I think we've agreed that I'll take the lead in this conversation. I want you there as a witness and support, but I'll ask the first questions. He hasn't met me, and we both know I can be utterly charming. Let me disarm him about his failure to investigate, and then we can both follow up with useful suggestions about how he might proceed."

Taylor winked conspiratorially. "Go get 'em, Tiger!"

❖

Precisely at nine thirty, a young woman showed Marilee and Taylor into the New Eden police chief's office. Though they were clearly his seniors in age, Chief Rufus Williams rudely failed to stand to greet them and waved them vaguely toward the two chairs facing his desk. "What can I do for you girls?" he asked.

Marilee winced. How could someone in his late fifties refer to two octogenarians as "girls"? If he'd been in her biology class, she'd have set him straight in a New York minute.

Marilee reached across the desk with an outstretched hand. "We haven't met, Chief. I'm a fairly new citizen of New Eden and a great admirer of this beautiful old town. My name is Marilee Connor, and you know Taylor Bradford, but you may not realize that before she came back here to practice law with her father, I knew her as runner-up for Sweetheart of the University of Texas, in 1962. Taylor, take a bow." There. Maybe that little tidbit would surprise the obviously set-in-his-ways officer and make him view Taylor in a different light.

Taylor curtseyed and, without speaking, sat down and turned to Marilee as if giving her the go-ahead.

"Chief, we've heard some disturbing reports from a friend of ours who's residing at the Silverado Nursing Home. She's been there only a short time, rehabbing from an accident, but some of her fellow residents have apparently been victimized by a cybercriminal, or criminals."

"Do tell, miss. I've heard some rumors about that situation myself but want to be sure I have my *facts* straight." He stared at her as if he doubted she understood the meaning of the word. "I assume you watched the popular TV series *Dragnet*, back in the 60s. I try not to miss a single rerun." He straightened up in his chair. "Just the facts, ma'am. That's my motto."

"Well, I'm simply a concerned citizen, not an investigative reporter. But I'll try to be as accurate and factual as possible," Marilee said, trying not to grit her teeth.

She hoped Taylor didn't have an *I told you so* gleam in her eyes. If she did, it would be difficult to keep herself from walking over and smacking her.

"Our friend at the nursing home, Dr. Edith Eyidah, first learned of the problem in the beauty salon at Silverado," she said.

"The beauty salon? That's about the most reliable place possible to gather information, I suppose." He smirked.

"Probably about as good as the barber shop," she retorted, "which I imagine is quite a popular and reliable spot."

The chief jerked and straightened his mouth into a thin line, then grunted. "Yep, missy. You may have a point there. And exactly what did your friend hear at the *beauty salon?*"

Taylor clutched the arms of the chair she was sitting in, and Marilee shook her head slightly. She could do this. He reminded her of an obnoxious student in introductory biology, and she'd handled several of them during her years of teaching.

She paused for emphasis and all but batted her eyelashes at the sour-faced man who was looking everywhere but at her. "One woman told our friend how she'd foiled a fake request for money from someone claiming to be her grandchild because she knew he was in Costa Rica and didn't have access to a phone."

The chief pulled out a pen and a notepad. "What is this woman's name, when did this happen, and how much money did the caller ask for?"

"Uh. I have no idea. I'm just telling you what she said. And what does it matter if no crime was committed?"

"Just the facts, ma'am. That's all I want and need." The chief pulled out an Altoid and stuck it in his mouth. "What can you tell me about an actual crime? That's what I'm in the business of dealing with here."

Marilee wanted to jerk the Altoid out of his mouth and throw it at him, but she restrained herself. "Another woman was in the beauty shop, waiting for a shampoo, and out of the blue, she burst out crying. Then, in a few minutes, she collected herself and whispered, as if she was ashamed, 'The same thing happened to me, and I paid up.'"

The chief finally scratched a line or two on an apparently brand-new notepad. "The victim's name, please."

Marilee had to take a deep breath to keep herself from screaming "I don't know!" She blew her breath out. "As I said, our friend who's a resident heard this conversation. I'm reporting a conversation that our friend who's a resident heard." She was tempted to ask Taylor to rescue her from this situation.

But suddenly, the obnoxious policeman laid his pen beside his pad. "How can I do my job with absolutely no information? I'm not a miracle worker, the last time I checked." He ran his tongue over his front teeth like he'd just finished eating an expensive steak dinner. Marilee had a wild urge to use his pen against him like a sword.

She cleared her throat and said in her most authoritative lecturer's tone, "Can we do anything to help you get to the bottom of all this?"

The chief finally made eye contact but pulled another Altoid from the nearby tin and slipped it into his mouth before he spoke with what she assumed he considered a properly stern tone. "Names would definitely have helped, but in fact, I do know what you're referring to. And"—he rolled the Altoid around in his mouth—"since the matter is already under investigation, I don't have anything more to say on the subject."

Marilee finally resorted to lowering her gaze, maybe squeezing out a tear. "Oh, Chief, if you could just give us and the residents at Silverado a little reassurance, it would go a long way to calming their fears. Those old people are terrified of either not helping someone who loves and needs them or being swindled in a con job that robs them of their savings. Can't you please tell us something?" She was flat out of feminine wiles.

The chief turned to her, his face reddening slightly. "Well, I suppose I could tell you that I intend to turn the case over to the Texas Rangers. We at the city level in Texas are unprepared to investigate phone and AI scams, since they typically originate out of the country. I don't have the authority or manpower to send detectives to China or wherever. And our citizens wouldn't stand for it if I did. We have no business trying to catch foreign criminals. Don't you agree, miss?"

Marilee returned his insult with a gracious expression. "Of course I understand, Chief. But from what I learned online last night, this isn't a matter of foreign hackers trying to break into corporate files. This is a local criminal trying to extort hard-earned savings from unsuspecting senior citizens. This type of crime would be small potatoes to the international crowd. And incidentally, I doubt the Rangers even have an AI or cybercrime department."

He flapped his hand in the air like he was swatting a fly. "Whatever. I can't talk about an ongoing investigation. And besides, what can you possibly know about this type of crime anyway? The Rangers help us out with crime scene investigations and cold cases, so I fully intend to ask them to check out this situation."

Marilee rose and turned to Taylor. "We've taken enough of this gentleman's time."

Without further prompting, Taylor jumped to her feet and followed Marilee out of the office. When they reached their car, Marilee already had her head between her knees before she heard Taylor say, "Well, that went well."

"Give me another minute." She visualized their peaceful backyard, birds flying around and butterflies soaring on a warm breeze. "I'm trying to keep my yogurt down. I can't believe that cretin holds a responsible position in this town."

"You did fine, sweetheart. At least maybe you have a better appreciation for what I've been up against trying to practice law here for the last fifty-odd years. You've done a great job this morning, but it's time for a professional to step in. Wouldn't you agree?"

Marilee raised her head tentatively. "Who do you have in mind?"

"Me, silly. I mean me! A mature Nancy Drew on the case."

CHAPTER V

Recruiting New Agents

Taylor pushed her feet on the floor of the front porch and set the old wooden swing in motion.

"Hey. Not so fast," Marilee said. "If you keep up that pace, you'll throw us out into the flowerbed."

Taylor dragged her feet across the hardwood porch to slow them. "Is that better?"

"It sure is. I thought we were supposed to be relaxing, not trying to catapult ourselves to the moon."

"You certainly tend to exaggerate. Always trying to slow me down."

"Well, I have to. Otherwise, you'd have us speeding through the rest of our lives so fast, we'd get injured or miss out on a lot of the beautiful moments we're supposed to be enjoying in our old age."

"Okay. I'll try. In fact, our new idea about being detectives may help. I might even give up lawyering altogether, and we could work together on what few sleuthing opportunities come our way."

They sat there, side by side, listening to the slow whoosh of the passing traffic and gazing at the waxy green leaves of the huge magnolia in the front yard. Finally, Marilee said softly, "Well, when you finally do slow down, you don't mess around, do you? Feel ready to discuss the nursing home situation we've gotten mixed up in?"

"I certainly do. We can handle this, can't we? Any ideas about what to do now?"

"Yes. First, we need to gather more information about what's going on out there. But we should be more subtle about it. Confronting the chief of police was too obvious. The good-old-boys' club is more alive and well here than I expected."

She frowned, and Taylor couldn't resist running her finger along the frown line on her forehead. "I love to watch the wheels turn in your pretty little head."

Marilee gently swatted her hand away. "Quit that. You sound as chauvinistic as that horrible police chief."

"Sorry." Taylor screwed up her face. "I'll try to do better."

"Okay, silly. I know you don't mean it. But I do have a brain in this pretty little head." Marilee smiled but grew silent again.

Taylor drew a deep breath and gazed out at the towering tree. It had to be right at eighty feet tall, and it certainly hadn't grown that tall overnight. Her stomach relaxed a bit. How wonderful to let someone else handle the strategizing for a change. Since her dad died ten years ago, she'd felt so isolated. Marilee was the first one who'd relieved that ache.

Marilee interrupted her musing. "I've got it!"

"What have you got?" Taylor straightened, sitting taller in the swing.

"We need to find someone to work part-time at the nursing home," Marilee said. "Someone a lot younger. They could go places and hear things we can't. And they'd definitely be more up to date on the latest technology, which keeps changing more quickly than we can possibly keep up with. They could even make some money, and you know how much teenagers need that nowadays, with having to pay for gas and snacks and new apps and so on."

"Hmm. We could have an undercover agent who helps us discover what's going on out there, and if any dangerous situations arise, we can step in and decide what outside authorities would be the best ones to handle them."

"That's a great idea, Marilee. I knew you could come up with a plan."

"Well, I do appreciate your confidence in me. Trying to talk to that chief of police sure didn't polish my self-image at all."

"Forget about him. He's a joke. We'll do everything we can to avoid crossing paths with him again."

Marilee brightened and squeezed her hand. "Thanks for that. I hope we're a great success just to show him how wrong he is about the situation at Silverado. Now we need to find someone willing to play along with our scheme."

She squeezed Marilee's hand in return. "Okay. And maybe I can be helpful in that area. I have a cousin who lives in town whose great-granddaughter would be perfect for what you have in mind. She's graduating from high school and might be free for the summer before she traipses off to college, or whatever she decides to do."

"That's more like it." Marilee swatted a bug that had landed on her arm. "Now, shall we retire to the sitting room, my dear? It's gotten dark, and these flying creatures are obviously attracted to my sweetness."

Taylor jumped up. "Of course. Retiring for the night sounds like a great idea. How does some TV sound, and dessert for you?"

"Well, I'd like to skip the TV—but not the dessert."

They sat side by side on the sofa, Marilee holding a bowl of ice cream. After Marilee finished the final spoonful, Taylor turned to her. "Why don't you tell me something about you that I ought to know?"

"Well, my husband and I never had children because that was my preference."

"Interesting. So many married women our age thought they wouldn't be a 'real woman' if they didn't have a baby."

Marilee agreed. "I did feel that type of pressure. We all did. But teaching science at the community college level, especially after I got involved in the emerging field of environmental science, excited and fulfilled me."

"How great. That must have been in, what, the seventies? I didn't know you were such a forward thinker." Taylor squeezed Marilee's arm.

"Did you ever miss having children, even though you never married?"

"Not a bit. I socialized mostly with male colleagues who left their wives at home to attend professional meetings." Taylor shrugged. "Nearly all my few female peers were unmarried and childless, so it was never much of an issue for me, either."

Marilee yawned. "Well, it's much too late in life to do anything about it, isn't it? And right now, I'm getting really sleepy. I've enjoyed this conversation, but I'd like to continue it when I can keep my eyes open." She kissed Taylor gently on the cheek. "Sweet dreams, dear one. Don't forget to call your cousin tomorrow about locating a teenager who can help us get on the inside at Silverado."

❖

"Hey, man. How's it going? I haven't seen or even talked to you in ages. Sorry I missed you at the annual get-together last week. What have you been up to?"

Taylor smoothed a wrinkle in her left sleeve as she listened to her cousin run through the highs and lows of his five children and their numerous offspring.

He was just a few months older than she was, and when they were teens, he'd loved to be around her, mainly because he was so girl crazy. He'd always told her how beautiful her girlfriends were.

Little did he know that she was just as attracted to a lot of them as he was. Of course, back then, she hadn't realized it either. She'd just enjoyed being with them, especially when they spent the night together talking and laughing. She'd never understood why the other girls didn't want to discuss anything but boys, though, when she just wanted to focus on them. It took a long time to understand what was going on.

"Yes, cuz," she said. He must have been chatting for quite a while and was probably wondering why she'd phoned him out of the blue like this. "Oh, uh, how's your great-granddaughter who's graduating? I got an announcement in the mail and plan to send her a present."

Again, he filled her in on all the news of that particular twig on the family tree.

Then, at last, she saw her opening. "Isn't her name Zooey?" She remembered it because of the old popular novel called *Franny and Zooey*. "Could you give me her contact information so I can get in touch with her in case she doesn't even know who I am? Teenagers get so wrapped up in their own little world they forget us stodgy old folks, but I would like to acknowledge her graduation."

"Sure thing, buddy." Soon he was back on the phone.

"Great," she said as his text arrived. "I really appreciate it."

As soon as they finished talking, Marilee walked into Taylor's office, carrying a glass of tea and one of ice water. "Hey," she said. "Thought you might want something to drink after that long phone call."

Taylor took her glass, sheepish. "Thanks. I appreciate it. Though my cousin is really the one who needs something to drink. He's always been talkative."

Marilee sat in a leather chair, her eyes shining. "But you got the necessary info. Right?"

Taylor sipped her water. "I certainly did. We need to buy a graduation gift, but we've found someone we can trust and who should be able to gather the information we need to crack our case wide open."

"Congratulations, Nancy Drew." Marilee held up her glass in a mock salute. "Looks like we're on our way to solving this nursing home hoax."

CHAPTER VI

Progress Undercover

"Work in a nursing home? With all those old people? That's not the way I want to spend my summer."

Zooey pushed her chair at the restaurant back, looking at her best friend Gloria. "Let's go. Maybe this was a mistake."

Taylor observed her young relative, who certainly could be direct.

"But we've just gotten our food," Gloria said. "I'd like to try out this place, and we've driven all the way to Tyler."

Using her napkin to muffle her voice, Zooey muttered to Gloria, "I thought we'd decided to get a summer job where we could be around a lot of other kids our age." Getting no response, Zooey turned to Taylor. "Sorry. I don't want to let you down, but working in a nursing home just couldn't be much fun. Since you're family, I'd like to do you this favor, and it was really nice of you to invite us to Tyler for lunch, but..."

Gloria gazed up at her but didn't budge. "This is the best pupusa I've eaten in a long time. Almost as good as the ones my abuelita back in El Salvador used to make. I'm not going anywhere until I finish mine," she said softly. She cut another piece with her fork and put it in her mouth. "Yum."

Zooey looked at her own plate.

Taylor gripped her water glass harder than usual, but Marilee didn't appear at all bothered by Zooey's remarks. Taylor tried to relax. Obviously, Zooey wasn't afraid to express herself forcefully. Taylor had never spent much time with her cousin's family, recalling Zooey mainly as a cute little girl at family picnics who never sat still and always said what was on her mind. Obviously, she'd developed those traits in spades.

Gloria, on the other hand, seemed immune to Zooey's impulsive behavior. She appeared more patient, subtle, maybe even more grown up, and able to hold her own ground with Zooey's blunt approach. Zooey had asked to include her because they were best friends, and the Senior Sleuths realized that having two agents undercover was even better than one.

Breaking the silence, Marilee finally asked, "What would it take for you to change your mind, Zooey?"

"Well, if you want me to work in a *nursing home,* I'd need to earn at least as much money as I can make part-time at some place like Schlotzsky's." She picked up her fork.

Taylor ate a bite of her pupusa. "And how much is that?"

"Ten dollars."

"An hour?" Marilee asked, sipping her iced tea.

"Of course." Zooey wrinkled her nose.

"When I was your age, I made sixty cents an hour, so ten dollars feels like a fortune to me."

Gloria spoke up. "Minimum wage is between seven and eight dollars right now."

"But we have a shortage of workers in town, Glo. So when I decide to earn some extra money, I always insist on being paid ten."

Taylor could almost read Marilee's mind. Zooey wouldn't miss a trick at the nursing home. "We'll see what we can work out, Zooey," she said. "Would you both consider working out there to help us?"

Zooey looked at Gloria, then asked, "What would you want us to do? I haven't been in one of those places very often, just sometimes to visit my great-grandmother before she died. It was so depressing there."

Taylor wished Marilee would come to her rescue but then said, "To be honest, Zooey, we'd like you and Gloria to be members of a new firm we're starting."

"What kind of firm?" Zooey finally took a bite of her own pupusa. "Hmm. This is pretty tasty."

"Kind of an investigation agency," Taylor said.

"We've decided to call it Senior Sleuths, so you two would be our junior sleuths," Marilee said.

"Investigation agency, like PIs on TV?" Zooey asked, putting down her fork.

"That's right. It would be just the four of us, and we have only one case so far," Taylor said.

"What kind of case? Finding out who stole somebody's box of Kleenex?" Zooey giggled at her own joke.

"A bit more serious than that." Taylor sipped her water. "But before we tell you what little we know, we'd like for you to carefully nose around and inform us if you find anything suspicious going on out there."

Zooey sat back in her chair, her eyes shining. "Really? Like what?"

"Has anything bad actually happened?" Gloria asked.

"Yes," Taylor said.

"But you want us to scope out this place and discover whatever it is for ourselves instead of telling us what to look for?"

"That's exactly what we want. That way, if you notice the same thing we've heard rumors about, we'll be certain we need to investigate whatever it is," Marilee said, gently elbowing Taylor.

"Got it. We'd be super alert and careful. By the way, can we pick what shift we want to work? I like to sleep late and stay up till midnight, so a late one would be good for me." Zooey was evidently checking to see if she was pushing the situation too far.

Taylor took a deep breath. "I really don't know. This isn't a lifelong commitment for you or the nursing home. But it will be good experience for you to apply and interview for the job on your own."

"Why's that?" Zooey asked. "I thought you'd help us get work."

"Well, in case somebody in the administration is a crook, we want our junior sleuths to be able to poke around there on their own without anyone realizing they're working with us. Does that make sense?"

Zooey and Gloria gazed at each other. "You're right. We're both adults. We can apply for a job by ourselves with no problem," Gloria said.

Taylor finished the last of her meal. "I agree. And I also imagine there's a rather high burn-out rate at any nursing facility, which leads to a lot of turnover." She wiped her mouth with her napkin. "And I'm certainly not worried about you two. I bet you could handle just about any situation."

"How about it, Glo? If I get a job there, will you get one, too? We'd be a great team and probably have fun snooping around trying to find out what's going on." Zooey rubbed her hands together. "I bet you could work in the office, since you've already had several business courses in high school."

Gloria tilted her head to one side, smiling faintly.

"You know, that's a good idea," Taylor said. "That way, Zooey could keep track of what goes on among the patients and staff, and Gloria could be on the lookout for irregularities in recordkeeping. You two would be a perfect match for this undercover assignment. If anything suspicious *is* going on, I'm sure you'd discover it quickly. Don't you agree, Marilee?"

Marilee's eyes danced. "I have no doubt that you two young women will be top-notch additions to our team, so we can quickly investigate any suspicious activity."

As they left the restaurant, Zooey said, "We'll drive out to Silverado as soon as we can and apply for part-time work. Then we'll be in touch. We've got both your numbers in our contacts."

As the girls sped away, Marilee said, "I have just one thing to say about this situation."

"What's that?" Taylor opened the car doors.

"I'm certainly glad I'm not the one who has to negotiate the terms of employment with those two."

"You and me both. I'd put my money on Zooey and Gloria any time. We've created a powerhouse team."

❖

"So, girls? How's the new job going?" Taylor asked five days later as she spotted Gloria and Zooey standing near the first hole of the local miniature-golf course in their sprawling city park.

"At least the food's pretty good out at Silverado," Zooey said. "And they let us snack on anything we can find in the kitchen between meals, so we're surviving." She stared at the wooded area. "It's sure deserted here at this old park. Where's Marilee?"

"Buying our tickets and picking up the equipment."

Soon, Marilee walked up, carrying four short golf clubs over one shoulder and four balls of different colors in her hand. "Ready to play? At least we have some privacy here, so you can tell us if you've noticed anything suspicious out at Silverado."

Standing at the first hole, Gloria said, "We were talking about the food a minute ago, Miss Taylor. The cooks out there are nice and do a good job, but we've noticed a few of them sneaking some supplies out in their oversized purses."

Taylor put her red ball on the small plastic pad at the start of the first hole. "Do they know about that in the office?" She couldn't keep from frowning as she asked.

"I'm not sure. But Zooey and I don't really blame them. Who could survive on the low pay those poor people get? Especially if they have a bunch of kids at home to feed."

"Speaking of that subject, are you two satisfied with your

pay?" Taylor hit her ball, which stopped at least three feet from the small hole directly in front of her.

"You bet," Gloria said. "We did better than we expected." She giggled, though Zooey kept a straight face. "With Zooey negotiating, Mrs. Hurd, the administrator who interviewed and hired us, didn't have a chance. In fact, after we were hired, Ms. Hurd took sick leave. I hope it wasn't our fault."

Zooey grinned as she dropped her black ball onto the plastic pad and took a practice swing in the air. "I just didn't give up. With the amount they charge those old people to live there, they could sure afford to pay two part-timers like us as much as a fast-food place would. And they should pay the rest of the staff a lot more, too."

"I'm sure you're right, Zooey," Taylor said as Marilee took her turn. "You should do well in whatever profession you choose. Do you have anything in mind?"

"Nothing set in stone." Zooey's serious expression made her appear more mature than Taylor had realized she was capable of being. "I'm really interested in the environment, sustainability, that kind of thing, but I also enjoy photography a lot. In fact, I earned quite a bit of spending money this year doing portrait shots of my friends who were graduating, and I didn't charge them nearly as much as a professional photographer would. It's good experience, and I enjoy it."

Taylor peeked at Marilee's ball, which had stopped much closer to the hole than hers had. "Maybe you can take some college courses in that area and see how you like it, Zooey." Taylor began to warm toward this girl/woman, who could shift from a silly teen to a thoughtful young adult instantly. Marilee and she had been just the same age as these two when they first met at the university.

Taylor stood beside Zooey silently as Gloria took her turn. After Gloria's ball stopped closer to the hole than anyone else's, Zooey blurted out, "Hey. We hoped we might find a few cute boys out there at the home, but no luck so far. And the women who live there have the same problem. In fact, some of them get their feelings really hurt because they believe one of the old codgers likes them best but find out he's doing the nasty with somebody else." She scrunched up her face. "Yuck. The second day I was there, I walked in on a situation like that. Gross!"

Next to her, Gloria giggled, and Zooey stopped talking.

"Did you knock first, Zooey?" Marilee was clearly having a hard time suppressing a grin.

"Of course! We have to do that." She scrunched up her face again. "I guess they were so carried away they didn't hear me, or maybe they didn't want to. Anyway, it was disgusting. I got out of there as fast as I could."

Marilee finally spoke in a soft, calm tone. "Well, those things aren't part of your job description, so try to ignore them. As young as you two are, it's natural for you to consider older people really different from you. But the way I care for someone now feels the same as it did when I was your age." She glanced at Taylor. "Maybe stronger. It's just the way people are made."

Zooey appeared caught between curiosity and disbelief.

Taylor lined up her ball and hit it toward the hole. It rolled up to one side but didn't fall in. "I know you said that some of the kitchen staff were stealing food, Zooey, but have you noticed anything more serious than that?" she asked, annoyed at her missed shot.

Leaning on her club, Gloria spoke up this time. "We wanted to make sure we were right before we mentioned this, but we keep hearing rumors about some of the old people getting phone calls that really upset them."

Taylor snapped to attention, her mind beginning to buzz. "Phone calls? What kind of phone calls?"

"Oh, I don't know. Those old folks were probably just blowing everything out of proportion," Zooey said. "If I didn't have anything to do but watch TV and play Bingo all day, I'd probably make up a bunch of stories, too, just to pass the time."

Taylor watched Marilee eye her ball, then stroke it easily

into the first hole. "Good job," she said, tightening her grip on her club.

"You just said something really important, Zooey," Taylor said as Gloria also knocked her ball into the first hole.

"What? About everybody blowing everything out of proportion?"

"No." Taylor tapped her ball in and scrawled the number three on her score card. She'd try to play better during the rest of the game. "About the phone calls."

"What? You mean there might be something to that story?" Zooey blurted out.

"Maybe." Taylor enjoyed teasing Zooey for a second, but then she patted her arm. "Our friend out there, Dr. Edith Eyidah, told us about the phone calls and said one poor woman even fell for a scam and lost a pile of money. That's why we decided to become senior sleuths and asked you two to join us."

"So we've passed our first test?" Gloria asked.

"You certainly have, with high marks," Marilee said, then headed toward the second hole.

❖

After they finished their golf game and were strolling back to their nearby vehicles, Marilee asked, "Are you girls enjoying your new adventure so far?"

Zooey didn't hesitate. "It's sure different. And I'm beginning to see older people in a new way."

"Like what?" Taylor half-smiled at Marilee.

"Well, they're not always grouchy and sad, like I'd thought they'd be." Zooey scratched her cheek. "They like to play games and put puzzles together, and they laugh and cut up a lot more than I ever imagined they would."

"And most of them are super nice," Gloria said. "They ask me questions and act like they're listening to my answers, like they're really interested in someone who grew up in another country but moved here at a young age. I'm glad my job is only partly in the office."

Zooey suddenly blurted out, "I'm actually glad I took this job, except..."

"Except what?" Taylor spotted her Ghia, parked a few spaces away from Zooey's white van. She'd evidently given Gloria a ride today.

"Except I was talking to a guy at work yesterday who gives me the creeps," Zooey said.

"The creeps?" Marilee asked. "What's that about?"

"Well, evidently he's been working there part-time for the last six months or so, and taking some courses at the college, too."

"What's wrong with that?" Taylor asked.

"Nothing. It's a good idea, but he was such a nerd in high school, I felt strange talking to him." Zooey shrugged. "Like his nerdiness might rub off on me."

Gloria giggled. "Nerdiness? What kind of word is that? And what do you mean—rub off on you? Do I know this guy?"

"I bet you do. Tall, skinny, greasy long hair, a real loner. He was a couple of grades ahead of us in high school." Zooey made a face.

"Nobody I remember fits that description, but what are you trying to say?"

"Nothing, really. I was just surprised to see him in the office. He works in the basement and probably has access to all their computers and can find personal information about all the residents at Silverado whether he's supposed to or not."

Taylor stopped walking and stared at Zooey. "What are you getting at? And why are you concerned about his having that kind of access?"

Zooey and Gloria locked eyes.

"John Gamble," they said at the same time.

"He got into a lot of trouble in his senior year at New Eden High when he was accused of hacking into the school mainframe and changing the grades of a lot of the kids who'd been mean to him," Gloria said. "Almost made our valedictorian lose his spot."

"He might be the one trying to swindle some of the old folks here," Zooey said.

"If he has the skill to access the school's computer system," Marilee said, "he could likely do the same thing at Silverado, couldn't he?"

Zooey and Gloria raised their fists above their heads. "We've broken the case wide open already, haven't we?" Zooey exclaimed. "Not bad for *junior* sleuths, is it?" The two of them high-fived each other. "This calls for a raise."

"Not so fast, girls," Taylor said calmly. "I don't mind rewarding you two, but aren't you two jumping to conclusions? What do you know about this guy John except one allegation about a high school prank?"

The girls stopped jumping around and crossed their arms. "But at least he's a pretty good suspect, isn't he?" Zooey asked.

"Maybe." Marilee frowned. "But Taylor has a good point. We can't go around condemning people without building a plausible case against them first."

Zooey told Gloria, "Rats. This detective work may not be as easy or as quick as I thought."

"But that's part of the reason I might like it," Gloria said. "We need to be smart and thorough and persistent. And patient. Then maybe we can find out who's being so mean to these nice people out there."

Marilee put her arm around the girls' waists. "I agree. You two will be the best junior sleuths ever. You just need practice and patience."

CHAPTER VII

New Hoaxes

Marilee and Taylor sat outside the Chat n Chew, waiting for their junior sleuths to join them and enjoying the unusually mild afternoon temperature. They knew full well that any day now, they'd be forced to hunker down inside because of the blazing heat that always invaded during late June.

Suddenly, Zooey's white van screeched to a halt in front of the cafe, and she and Gloria jumped out and hurried up the front sidewalk. "We're on our way to work but wanted to stop by and let you know the latest." All four went in and moved to an empty side room. Taylor took drink orders and soon returned with four large cups.

Taylor studied them as she distributed the refreshments. "What's up, guys?"

"Well, last night right before we left, one of the staff members that's about to quit her job there told me, all secret-like, something about Mrs. Richards—you know her, that very wealthy woman who used to live in that huge two-story brick mansion on West Main. She has to be in her late nineties."

"Yes, Gloria," Zooey said. "Everybody in town knows about her. Her husband was a head honcho at the local brick plant and made millions from that business."

"But what about Mrs. Richards?" Marilee asked.

"Well, nobody knows anything about this except a few of the staff, but here's what I heard when I was in and out of some of the offices there." Gloria cleared her throat. "Yesterday, the girl who knocks on everybody's door each afternoon about three thirty to read them the menu for that night and write down what they want to eat found Mrs. Richards crying, a lot."

"What was wrong with her?" Marilee sounded full of sympathy, even though the woman was known as being as unpleasant as a house fly buzzing around the room.

"The girl—I can't remember her name—said Mrs. Richards was mumbling something about a phone call she'd gotten and how many thousands of dollars it would cost her to get somebody in her family out of trouble, or else that person would set somebody's house on fire." Gloria had spoken louder and louder as she talked, but then she stopped abruptly and leaned back in her chair, her silence echoing through the quiet, empty room.

"My goodness," Marilee said. "The poor old thing. I feel sorry for her."

Taylor spoke up. "Well, she's not an easy person to feel sorry for, but I *am* concerned. No one, especially somebody as old as she is, should be victimized by that kind of threat."

Zooey had sat quietly through Gloria's revelation, but now she took center stage. "And she's not the only one that has something bad happening to her. I heard another story last night, too, just before I got off work, and it's really hush-hush." She straightened the collar of her T-shirt. "Mr. Yandle, who used to be my great-granddaddy's school bus driver back before all the kids had their own car—yes, Gloria, that's right, and my great-aunt said only a few boys had their own car when she was in school, if you can believe that." She shrugged as if doubting the reliability of that information. "Anyway, Mr. Yandle's over a hundred years old now, and he's upset about something, too.

Several of the old folks are still getting weird phone calls that have to do with money, and nobody knows what to do about them."

Taylor sipped her ice water, then stopped and cradled her chin in her right hand. "Hmm. These threats sound like the type of scam we've been on the lookout for."

"Elders seem like a strange target for scams like this," Marilee said. "Sounds like something young, rich techies would be victimized by. Of course I don't know much of anything about it, so maybe the crooks are focusing on us uninformed old people."

"Well, you're probably right," Taylor said. "Cybercrime and phone scams have been around since everybody started using computers and cell phones, but it's gotten more and more sophisticated. And the addition of AI to the mix has made it almost impossible to know if you're communicating with someone you know who's in trouble, or if some crook is trying to rob you. I'm afraid that's what's happening to old people like Mrs. Richards and Mr. Yandle."

"You're right," Zooey said. "We discussed it in some of my classes at school this past semester, but we're all so used to computers we weren't worried about being able to defend ourselves." She seemed to be seeing Taylor and Marilee for the first time. "Y'all really didn't have anything nearly as sophisticated as the computers and smartphones that we do, did you? Wow."

"We had pencils and ink, pens and paper. And our brains. In fact, you'd be amazed how much you can do with equipment like that." Taylor smiled to show she was kidding, but she halfway meant what she'd just said. Honestly, she wasn't sure if all this technology was a blessing or a curse.

Zooey glanced at her smartwatch and drained her glass. "Wow. It's almost four o'clock. We better get a move on, or we'll be late. Thanks for the drinks. Come on, Gloria."

And as suddenly as they'd arrived, they jumped into Zooey's van and roared away.

"Whew," Marilee said. "Did we ever have that much energy?"

"I imagine so. But we didn't have any way to spread it around as fast as they do." Taylor got up. "Ready to go? I need a nap."

"You bet, although I may read in my recliner rather than sleep. I'll be much better equipped to sleuth after a brief rest." Marilee hooked her arm through Taylor's as they left the café.

❖

Taylor's phone beeped early the next morning. "I need to change my ringtone to something more soothing," she muttered to herself as she held the phone to her ear. "Hello. Oh, hi, Edith. That's okay. I'm just sleeping a little late this morning." She studied her digital alarm clock. "Well, make that a lot late. You what? Slow down. I'm sorry, but Marilee and I have an important appointment today and can't make it out to Silverado until later. We can't miss this meeting, and we need to leave as soon as we can, so we won't be late. I'm glad you woke me up. But listen— okay? Try to take it easy. We'll stop by about three this afternoon. All right?"

On her way downstairs, Taylor saw Marilee emerge from her room. "Who just called?" Marilee asked. "Thank goodness they did, or I'd still be asleep."

"Oh, Edith was upset about something that a new resident just told a group of them at the nursing home's beauty parlor. I wish we had time to go check it out this morning."

"I do, too. I hate to leave Edith when something upsetting is happening at Silverado, but we shouldn't miss this opportunity to investigate Barb's suspicious new benefactor. We're so late, let's pick up a bacon, egg, and cheese biscuit from McDonald's and hit the road."

They started down the stairs, holding on to the railing and concentrating on where they stepped.

❖

After a mad scramble to get out the door, Marilee and Taylor settled into the two-hour ride to Dallas. "Thanks for letting me drive, Taylor. The Rogue is much more pleasant for longer trips. Don't you agree?"

"I guess so," Taylor muttered. "You can fight the traffic while I consider what to ask my friend. You did put the address in Google Maps, didn't you?"

"I certainly did, but you can't hear the directions because they feed directly into my hearing aids. I'll be fine until we get near Dallas. I don't know Oak Cliff very well. If I seem to be shushing you, it's just because the guidance system is talking to me. Until then, think out loud about what we need to ask your friend."

"Sure. I've already told you she lives in Oak Cliff and has since childhood. She was one of my roommates in law school, and I visited her home a couple of times back then. We kept in touch as colleagues. Not many other women practiced law during our early years."

"I know what you mean. A few taught science courses in high school, but fewer in the college, and almost none at the university."

"When Shannon mentioned Oak Cliff the other day, this friend's name came to mind. On a hunch I called her and found out her daughter was in the same high school as Shannon and the guy who's now New Eden's police chief. Small world, right?"

"Absolutely. But Dallas is huge. What luck to find our suspect in a haystack that big."

"I agree, but Oak Cliff's special. It's south of the Trinity River, and most of Dallas is to the north and east. It's an especially beautiful part of the county, with a gently rolling landscape. My friend's family lived in one of the original homes in the area, with beautiful trees and landscaping. Very lovely."

"Sounds like Bradford's Arbor to me."

"Quite a bit, especially back then. Nowadays, while those beautiful original areas are still there, it features restaurants and entertainment venues. And the population's much more diverse."

"I'm just guessing our police chief didn't come from the posh section."

"You could be right," Taylor said. "And I'll want to see if my friend knows anything about his family background."

"Okay. Write that down. What else do we need to ask? By the way, are we taking her out to eat? It sounds like we could find plenty of places nearby."

"Definitely, but my friend has serious mobility problems and has invited us to eat at her house. I imagine she has plenty of help, so we won't be inconveniencing her. In fact, she sounded like she'd enjoy some company. So I've got that main item— to ask about the chief's background. And obviously we want to know if the chief, my friend's daughter, and Shannon had any connection. What else?"

"We should let the conversation flow and follow where it leads. Can you check my phone and tell me how long it'll be before we get there. I hope we're not late."

"According to Google Maps, our ETA is 11:29. In ten minutes, we'll be one minute early, which I'm sure we can make up by struggling up the front steps. You deserve a medal for quick dressing this morning, Marilee. I'm impressed."

"Thanks. Now comes the part where I have to listen to the GPS tell me what to do. You're free to enjoy the ride without further conversation." Marilee pushed her glasses up on her nose and followed the directions given by her navigation device.

As predicted, ten minutes later, they pulled up in front of a huge two-story craftsman mansion.

"Here we are, right on time. Let's see what your friend has to tell us about our first suspect as Senior Sleuths."

A young man opened the door and, after they identified themselves, said, "Come right in. We've been expecting you." He showed them into the living room, where their hostess sat in her wheelchair, eagerly studying them.

Taylor hurried over and hugged her. "How good to see you. You look great! How have you been feeling? Oh, before you answer that, how about I introduce my friend, my current work partner, and my undergraduate roommate at UT, Marilee Connor. Marilee, meet my law school roommate, Tillie Swanson."

Marilee walked over and took the woman's hand. "It's so good to meet you, Tillie. Since Taylor and I are working on our first case together, we appreciate your agreeing to see us. And as two of Taylor's former roommates, I'm sure we have a lot to talk about, but that can wait."

"It's so good to see you both," Tillie said. "Yes. Let's eat first and do some business. We can save the reminiscing for dessert. How's that sound?"

Tillie turned back to the young man who'd greeted them. "Will you let the kitchen know we're ready for them to serve? Thanks. Ladies, follow me to the dining room."

"Need any help?" Taylor asked.

"No, thank you," Tillie replied. "I've been in this chair long enough to have the house modified for my mobility. See, there's no carpet to slow me down, nor furniture in the way of maneuvering from room to room. And here's the dining room, anyway. Why don't you two sit on either side of me. It makes it easier for me to hear if you're close."

Polite chatter followed as the three of them were served lunch and began their meal.

After several bites and the appropriate appreciative words, Taylor spoke up. "We don't want to abuse your time, Tillie, and I have a list of the most critical items we want to ask. But first let me sketch in the reason for our visit. Marilee and I are both retired. After my father and her husband died, we reconnected, and recently she's moved into one of my spare bedrooms." She reached over and squeezed Marilee's hand. "We enjoy each other's company."

"That's so nice, Taylor," Tillie said. "I've always hoped you'd find someone special. All you've ever seemed to do is work."

"Well, I'm tapering off from lawyering, but we want to find something challenging to do together. In fact, an old friend of ours from the university just turned up in a rehab facility in New Eden. She's doing well, but some of her fellow residents are evidently the victims of extortion schemes. We went to the local police for help, but the chief turned us down flat."

"Flat doesn't half cover it," Marilee said. "The chief was rude beyond belief. But we can't say we hadn't been warned. In a casual conversation with Taylor's new neighbor, we met her younger friend. The two of them had just returned from a river cruise in France, for which the younger woman paid both fares. However, her generosity didn't extend to our police chief. When we mentioned that we planned to ask him for help at the nursing home, she lost it. She clearly distrusts that man and warned us not to expect any help—or respect—from him."

"She was right," Taylor admitted. "But her extreme reaction raised a red flag. In fact, the woman nearly fainted. Could the two of them have had a legal clash? Or maybe she'd profited from some type of criminal activity? Then I discovered that both the woman and the chief used to live in Oak Cliff. So, I thought of you."

"It's kind of you not to call me the oldest living Oak Cliff resident, though I'm certain to be in the upper one percent. But it so happens that my age is a real advantage when it comes to things that happened a while back. And the situation that involves those two isn't all that long ago."

"So you do know them!" Marilee said. "Tell us more."

"As it happens, my daughter, our only child, went to junior high and high school with both those kids. I'll call them Shannon and Bubba, because that's what my daughter called them. I checked with her before you got here, and here's what we remember.

"My daughter and Shannon went to a private elementary school together. They weren't best friends, but they knew each other. Each one had begged to attend public school, so they ended up in the same junior high not far from here. Bubba had gone to a public elementary school in the neighborhood, so it was expected for him to go to the nearby junior high, too. That's how they all ended up in the same seventh-grade class, though in different homerooms. But the trouble didn't start until Shannon and Bubba got to high school, where they were in the same homeroom. My daughter wasn't in theirs, so her information is all hearsay, but it was so widely known I'm pretty sure it's generally true."

"We'll double-check any actionable info you give us. But you can certainly help us get started," Taylor said.

"Can you tell from what I've already said that all three of the kids came from the same area in Oak Cliff? Well, they did. And I suppose it's obvious that most of the families around here are pretty well off. That was certainly true of the parents of Shannon and of Bubba. I met them at PTA meetings, and they all appeared to be perfectly nice and respectable."

"Well, that'll teach me to stereotype," Marilee said. "I'd guessed he was from the wrong side of the tracks."

"No. The problem was hormones. Bubba took one look at Shannon when she appeared in his tenth-grade room and fell ferociously in love. Apparently, during that first year of high school, Shannon was unaware that she'd become the object of his affection. But in the spring of their junior year, as school dances offered Bubba opportunities for nearness, he started asking her out. At first, she declined, politely, but he persisted. When the junior prom loomed, and no one else had asked her, Shannon capitulated and accepted his invitation.

"He went all out: a wrist corsage of carefully coordinated colors, a whole day spent cleaning and buffing the family car. He even polished his best shoes to an amazing shine. None of that helped.

"When they got to the dance, Shannon immediately joined her girl gang, leaving Bubba without a date. By mid-evening, another boy had noticed her, and she divided the rest of the time between him and the girls. She must have known she was being rude, so she did find Bubba in time for the last dance, and they went home together. But it was too late. Bubba clearly felt humiliated and evidently spent the next eleven months plotting his revenge.

"When it came time for the senior prom, Bubba waited until just a few days before the dance to invite her. As expected, she turned him down, saying she already had a date."

Tillie paused to ask if they wanted anything more to eat. They impatiently declined and urged her to finish her tale of adolescent love.

"My daughter didn't know all the details, but the whole school was buzzing that Monday about what Bubba did to Shannon at the prom. The way the rumor mill told it, Bubba had brought another girl to the dance that no one knew, someone from a private high school. The couple looked like they were having a great time, showing off their dance moves and flirting ostentatiously. Shannon reportedly rose to his bait by appearing fascinated with her own date. So she was clearly surprised when Bubba crossed the gym floor to ask her for the last dance of the prom. Perhaps imagining that this was his way of apologizing, she accepted. But as soon as she took his hand, she felt something sticky and realized he'd covered his palms with ketchup.

"Almost immediately he touched her dress, her hair, and her back. Then, as she ran from the gym crying, he screamed maniacally."

Tillie paused, then took a long drink of water. "I know it

sounds like the plot of a Stephen King movie that had come out a few years before. Bubba had evidently been inspired. So, this middle-class kid from a nice family showed himself to be vindictive and nasty. And during the next few days, several girls came forward to admit that he'd treated them badly, even bullied them. He didn't return to school and had to go to summer school to graduate. Shannon took her final exams at home, with a doctor's excuse for not returning to campus."

"That certainly explains why she would try to discourage us from asking our police chief for help," Marilee said.

"I have just one question," Taylor said. "Why did Shannon want to help an elderly woman like Barb? I presume Shannon's family had some money. Is there more to it than that?"

"Yes! And this is the best part," Tillie said. "Shannon's husband died young, and she inherited his money, but several years later, while visiting her own mother in a nursing home, she realized the resident across the hall was the mother of the boy who'd caused her so much agony in high school. She gathered her courage, introduced herself to the woman across the hall, and found that the older woman had followed Shannon through the years, hoping their paths would cross. She and her husband had been appalled to learn of their son's conduct, but they'd never been able to defuse his rage toward Shannon and women in general. So they'd lost contact with him and planned to leave their estate to Shannon to use to improve the lives of women. And that's exactly what she was doing when she took your neighbor on a river cruise. How's that for a happy ending?"

"It sounds almost too good to be true," Taylor said.

"I know what you mean," Tillie replied. "But I had my daughter check out the accuracy of Shannon's story. She's legit. One of those remarkable women who use the means available to them to make the world a better place. And she lives near you now. Aren't you glad?"

"More than glad. And relieved. We were on the verge of

investigating her for criminal extortion. It's such a relief that our first suspect turned out to be a philanthropist rather than a crook. Don't you agree, Marilee?"

"You're right. Tillie, you've helped us avoid an embarrassing mistake. You may hear from us Senior Sleuths again. I hate to break up the party, but we have a three o'clock appointment back in New Eden. We'll have to postpone our dessert session on what it's like to be Taylor's roommate. But I do hope we can have that conversation. Soon."

❖

"Where have you two been?" Zooey asked as she rushed up to Taylor and Marilee that afternoon when they pushed through the front door at Silverado. "It's been crazy here, and Gloria's got a ton of stuff to tell you."

"Okay. Calm down, girl. Why don't Marilee and I walk down to Edith's room like we're just paying her a visit? It's only ten after three, so we're here at a time that won't make anybody suspicious. Why are you here early, anyway? I thought you didn't start till four."

Zooey shrugged. "Gloria called me, worried, and said she's been trying to do her work in the office and help Edith not be too upset. She needed reinforcements."

"Edith phoned this morning going on about something happening at the beauty shop, but we already had plans for today, so I'm afraid I kinda blew her off," Taylor said.

"I'll let her tell you," Zooey said. "Why don't you two go down to her room and hear what she has to say, and I'll do some of my chores. I'll be working nearby if you need me."

"Good idea," Marilee said. "We appreciate your taking care of things while we were out of pocket, Zooey."

Zooey beamed and walked tall as she left them.

"That girl's growing up in front of our eyes," Taylor said.

"She's nothing like the brat who wasn't interested in anything except money and boys when we met. I'm impressed."

Down the hall, Taylor knocked on Edith's door, surprised when it opened almost immediately. "What the heck? Have you been standing right there all day? You know you're supposed to stay off your legs as much as you can."

"Thank goodness you've come. Finally. This has not been a quiet day at Silverado."

They helped Edith back into her big, comfortable lounge chair and got her a glass of water. "Sip some of this, Edith," Marilee said. "Then tell us what's happened to upset you so much."

Edith smoothed her curly gray hair away from her face and polished off the water in one long gulp. "Whew," she finally said, her shoulders hunched up almost to her ears. "I can't remember when I've felt so useless. Being around folks who are in distress and not being able to do a thing about it is terrible. This has been a day I'd rather forget."

"We're all together now, and I bet we can make sense of this. But would you like me to help you with your hair first, Edith?"

"Yes, thank you. It's early to get ready for bed, but I want to put this new satin bonnet on, and I just can't hold my arms up long enough to get it right. They feel so weak."

Marilee picked up the ends of her satin night cap and brought them around Edith's head, tying the ends in a secure bow on top of her head. "Better? Want to tell us about what's been going on?" she asked, noticing that Edith's shoulders had dropped a bit.

Edith motioned for another glass of water and then nodded after she took a long drink. Taylor and Marilee sat in the two guest chairs in the room, and slowly Edith settled into a relaxed position. "Well, I was in the beauty parlor this morning, just like I am every Wednesday, when all of a sudden old Mrs. Gray, the one with the purple hair, burst in, late to her appointment." Marilee nodded, but apparently Edith didn't notice her response.

"I'd just gotten my hair washed and was sitting there with a towel wrapped around my head, when out of the blue, Mrs. Gray started weeping noisily."

"What on earth was the matter with her?" Marilee leaned closer and took one of Edith's hands.

"We couldn't make sense of what she was trying to say for a while, because she was crying and talking at the same time." Edith looked like she might tear up, too.

Finally, Edith said, "Mrs. Gray told us a terrible story about her grandson calling her yesterday. I've never felt so sorry for anyone in my life."

"Well, what exactly did he say, Edith?" Taylor asked.

"That he was minding his own business, just walking down the street, when some guys jerked him right off the pavement where he lives in Florida and accused him of robbing a liquor store and raping a young woman!"

Taylor was startled. That was what Edith had been trying to tell her this morning, and she'd just brushed her off because she had her mind on their trip to Oak Cliff. "Well, what happened then?"

"They threw him in the back seat of a car and took him to an office, where a man ordered him to call someone who could help him straighten out the mess. Rather than upset his mother, who's been sick, he called his grandmother, begging her to do whatever the man told her to do."

"What were the instructions?" Taylor asked in her best lawyer voice.

"The man said it would cost her twenty-five thousand dollars, but if Mrs. Gray sent it immediately, he could get all the charges against her grandson dropped."

"And what did she do?" Marilee asked gently, squeezing Edith's hand.

"She was panicked, so she called her banker and gave him clear instructions about what to do."

"This Mrs. Gray sent them twenty-five thousand dollars?"

"Yes. The poor old thing. She'd inherited it when her husband died, but that just about wiped her out. She said she can't afford to stay here any longer."

Edith squeezed Marilee's hand so hard, Marilee had to let go. "But that's not the end of the story."

"Tell us the rest," Taylor said.

"Later, Mrs. Gray phoned her daughter to talk to her about the situation, and her daughter informed her that the grandson she was talking about was upstairs asleep in his bed, where he'd been for the past three days, recovering from some minor surgery on his leg."

"Oh, no," Marilee said. "So it was definitely a scam."

"Exactly," Edith said. "And I don't know what has upset Mrs. Gray the most—losing all that money or falling for such an obvious lie."

Taylor rubbed her forehead. "It's the fault of AI. And without computers, we would never have had something like that."

"Oh, don't be such a Luddite, Taylor," Marilee said.

"I agree that modern technology may have led us in some undesirable directions, but I'm not quite that bad." Taylor winked at Marilee, yet Edith didn't smile.

"What's wrong, Edith?" Marilee asked. "I thought you'd finished your terrible story."

"I haven't told you the worst part yet."

"You didn't fall for a scam, too, did you?" Taylor asked, trying to make a joke.

"No. But I made the big mistake of telling one of my fellow residents about it, which upset her, too."

"Well, that's not too bad, is it?" Marilee asked.

"It is when Miss Davis, the assistant administrator of the place, overhears you and accuses you in no uncertain terms of spreading rumors."

"Even if they're true?" Marilee frowned.

"Yes. She informed me that it's bad for morale, and if I have anything like that to report, I should speak only to her, not to any of the other residents."

Taylor huffed. "Well, I might have something to say about that to that know-it-all Miss Davis, even if I've never met her."

Marilee stood up and stretched her back. "And I might suggest that we keep all this to ourselves until we get a better idea of what's going on around here. Agreed?" She looked at Taylor and Edith.

"Agreed," they both said.

We have a lot of business to discuss, and this is clearly not a safe place for discussion," Marilee said. "It's about time we opened the Senior Sleuths' office for business—and pleasure. Edith, will you be ready for an outing by Saturday evening? Why don't we plan to have a work session at our home starting at four o'clock, with dinner following? How does that sound?"

Edith brightened. "That gives me a goal to work toward. I'll plan on feeling well enough to be transported to Bradford's Arbor by Saturday afternoon. It won't be a late night, will it?"

Taylor and Marilee answered in unison. "No!"

"We don't do late nights," Marilee said. "In fact, we'll probably have you back here before dark. How does that sound?"

"It's very satisfactory to be among age-peers." Edith smiled.

CHAPTER VIII

Joining Forces

"I'll get it. It must be the girls," Marilee said as the doorbell chimed. She removed the dishcloth she'd tied around her waist as an apron and returned it to Taylor's part-time private chef, Greta. "As soon as Taylor gets back with Edith, we'll be ready to start the meeting. You can bring in the refreshments when you get a minute."

Leaving the kitchen for the entrance foyer, she heard Zooey and Gloria on the front porch. "Can you believe this place?" Zooey asked. "I know my family's somehow related to Taylor, but I can't remember ever being inside her house. I've always wondered what it looks like."

"Wow. It must take lots of money and people to keep it up," Gloria said.

As Marilee opened the front door, Zooey jerked her head back. "We thought Miss Taylor would be here. Not you," she said. "Isn't that her Karmann Ghia in the back?"

"Oh, yeah. Taylor went to pick up Dr. Edith, and the Ghia is hard for Edith—for anybody—to get into." She hoped the girls didn't sense that it bothered her that Taylor, at her age, would still drive a vehicle better suited to these teenagers than to an octogenarian. She opened the door wider. "Come on in, you two. Can I show you around Bradford's Arbor a little?"

After she ushered them into the glass-paned foyer, she gestured toward the rear of the house. "Back there is where Greta is working her kitchen magic. Chicken cordon bleu, potatoes dauphinoise, and asparagus are on the menu for tonight. How does that sound?"

"Fine, I guess. What kind of chicken is that?" Gloria asked. "And do you really have a private chef?" She studied the bright foyer, wide-eyed when she came to the grandfather clock.

"It's just a fancy French name for baked chicken breast stuffed with ham and cheese, Gloria. And the potatoes are cooked in cream. I hope you'll like them." Smiling, Marilee said, "And Miss Taylor only brings the chef in when we have important guests."

Gloria rocked back and raised her eyebrows, one hand pointing to her chest, as if amazed to be considered an important guest.

"I'm pretty hungry already," Zooey added, her tense face appearing more relaxed after Marilee clarified what the main dish was. "I'll be glad to eat whatever you serve, Miss Marilee."

From the way they were talking, Marilee recognized the girls were on their best behavior.

She led them toward the formal living room. "Greta will be bringing us something to nibble on, so we can have a meeting before dinner. It's four now, and we've planned to eat at six to give us plenty of time to catch up on all the details of your undercover work at Silverado."

Zooey elbowed Gloria, both of them staring at the gleaming black grand piano in the corner. Gloria swallowed hard as she studied it, then the imposing family portrait in its ornate gilt frame hanging on the wall behind a red-velvet Victorian couch, slightly shaking her head. Marilee could relate. She'd grown up in a lower-middle-class home in Texas and guessed that Zooey's and Gloria's upbringings were closer to hers than to Taylor's.

She let the girls take their time strolling around, then said,

"Let me show you the working side of this house, where Taylor has her law practice. Upstairs, of course, are three bedrooms and a small sitting room with a sleeper sofa." Marilee led the way through the elegant living room into the reception area for Taylor's law office.

"Wow!" Zooey exclaimed as she entered the room. "What totally cool windows. It's like they take the place of the whole outside wall. It fills the room with golden light."

"I really like the dark wood paneling," Gloria said. "And the paintings of bluebonnets are beautiful." She and Zooey both stopped at the beautiful old walnut desk where Lois sat.

After Marilee introduced them, Lois said, "Welcome to the office of Bradford and Bradford, you two. Taylor just texted that she's picked up Dr. Edith and should be here soon. Would you like to wait for her in the conference room?"

"Sure," Gloria said, moving more naturally now, and the four of them walked toward the rear of the office, where a solid wood door led to a large area. "What a beautiful room. Check out all these books. Wow." She hesitated behind one of the chairs surrounding the mahogany table. "This table is gorgeous, too, especially with all the intricate designs cut into the wood."

"Go ahead," Marilee said. "Make yourselves comfortable. Sit wherever you like, but let's leave the head of the conference table for Miss Taylor. She likes to believe she's in charge. And just so you'll know, the door on the left leads to Taylor's private office, and the one on the right connects to a powder room and the hallway to the kitchen." Just as she finished, the right-side door opened with Greta carrying in a loaded tray, which she set on a side table. After she offered to serve them, all three accepted a cucumber sandwich and a glass of lemonade.

"Why don't you leave the refreshments on this table so they'll be easy to reach. We've got lots of ground to cover before we can have dinner," Marilee said, as the chef left the room. "Oh, great! Here come Edith and Taylor."

Lois held the door open while Taylor pushed Edith's wheelchair into the room. "Don't get up," Edith said. "I'd rather have you help me sit in the chair next to you."

Marilee poured a lemonade and set it in front of Dr. Edith. "Sandwich?"

"No, thanks. I hear we have an elegant meal coming, and I want to savor every bite." She licked her lips. "The food at Silverado is perfectly fine, but it's a little ordinary. I'm finally feeling well enough for something special."

Marilee looked toward Taylor. "How about we take a minute to introduce ourselves, just to make sure we're clear about who we are and what our objectives are."

Taylor cleared her throat. "Why don't you start, Lois?"

Lois, who sat to the right of Taylor, as if she wanted to be in easy reach, straightened the papers that lay in front of her. "Glad to. I'm Lois Ennis, Miss Taylor's executive assistant and legal secretary." She briefly met the gaze of each of them, as if giving them an individual welcome. She appeared totally at ease with Taylor yet managed to convey her respect for Taylor's status as her employer. "I'm the granddaughter of Miss Taylor's former housekeeper, June Johnson, who grew up in the garage apartment in back. Though she doesn't live there anymore, she still comes to help do light housework and serve dinner when Miss Taylor's entertaining. I'll be taking notes during our meeting, and then—though I'd like to stay for dinner—I need to pop back out to my room. When I returned to New Eden after college, Miss Taylor invited me to live here, so I'd be close to work and save money. But I'm not far from graduate school in Tyler, either. In fact, I have an online course that's meeting tonight."

"Online course? What are you taking?" Zooey asked.

Was she considering college? Marilee realized she knew very little about this young woman's interests and ambitions.

Lois responded to Zooey. "As much as I like the law, I'm in the social work program at UT-Tyler, studying to do something that combines my legal experience with my interest in community development."

Taylor chimed in. "I don't know what I'll do without Lois. She backs me up, makes it possible for me to travel, and has about a million good ideas a minute. But she has contributions to make in a wider field than my dwindling law practice. Thanks, Lois. Who's next?"

Zooey spoke up. "I'll go. I'm Zooey, Miss Taylor's relative somehow and a graduate—last week—of New Eden High School. I'm not totally sure where I'll go to college, but I plan to study either photography or environmental science wherever I end up."

Aha. Environmental science. That wasn't even an approved major when I was at UT. Marilee envied these young women for having so many new, interesting career opportunities.

"I want to understand more about what's happening to our planet and document it with photography," Zooey said. "The way things are going now, there may not be any more people or plants or records of what went wrong if we don't get our act together right away." Her eyes were flashing.

Edith beamed with approval. "Maybe the future's in safer hands than I realized."

"What good news!" Marilee said. "Biology was my major, and I have my master's degree in education, with a concentration in biological sciences. I'm sure you're already familiar with the area's junior colleges, and UT-Tyler has an upper-level program called Environment, Biodiversity, and Conservation. Plus, it's close. You should talk to Lois about going there. Gloria, what's your story?"

Gloria gulped, clutching the arms of the chair she was sitting in. "Well, I'm in this group because Zooey and I are best friends. We met when I came to this country eight years ago from El Salvador." She glanced at Zooey with obvious affection. "I would have gone into the fifth grade back home, but they put me back a year here, to improve my English."

Zooey nodded, and Gloria appeared to draw strength from their connection.

"Zooey was one of the few who would even talk to me at first, and having a friend to practice English with has really made a difference. I owe her a lot, and she's introduced me to some interesting activities. So when she asked me to join her in working at Silverado, I couldn't say no."

Zooey took a sip of lemonade from the glass in front of her and motioned for Gloria to do the same.

Her voice stronger, Gloria took a deep breath, obviously more confident. "I also graduated this year. Finally. I'm already nineteen, but I'm not sure if college is my next step." Her voice weakened. "My family is struggling to be able to open a Salvadoran restaurant downtown like the one Miss Taylor and Miss Marilee treated us to in Tyler the other day, and I'm sure they're counting on my help."

She glanced at Zooey again, who appeared laser-focused on her. "But it may be possible for me to go to a nearby junior college part time. If I get to do that, I'll probably take more business courses, so I can use what I learn to help out with the bookkeeping and paperwork for the restaurant." Suddenly she stopped and checked in with Zooey. "Did I say enough?"

Zooey looked at the others and nodded, and Gloria took a deep breath, clearly relieved. "I guess you could mention that we both graduated in the top quarter of our class," Zooey added.

Gloria blushed faintly and dipped her head.

Just then, Edith chimed in. "Well, it's clear that I'm among bright people." She beamed. "I'm so glad to see that America's young people haven't all turned to social media or drugs."

Marilee couldn't help but grin.

"Okay, my turn. My name is Edith Eyidah, and I am a physician. I spent my entire career practicing medicine in Ghana. I married a Ghanaian man, and we raised our three children there. I am back home now because I recently fell and broke my hip.

That got my attention, and I just felt like it was time to come back to Texas."

Marilee turned to Edith. "Why don't you share some of your story with the girls? I imagine they'd be interested."

"*I* certainly am," Gloria said, then blushed again when they all turned to her expectantly.

Edith gazed at everyone warmly. "I knew Taylor and Marilee from my first week at UT-Austin—we met at the Y, painting signs for a protest demonstration in front of the theaters on the Drag. That's the main street beside the campus, for those of you who don't have orange blood in your veins." Edith laughed softly at this reference to the university's school colors of orange and white, then spoke directly to Gloria and Zooey. "I know it must be almost impossible for you youngsters to understand what it was like here sixty years ago."

Edith took a deep breath, as if trying to organize her memories. "I got a good foundation for medical school at UT but had go to school in Tennessee to get my MD, because all the medical schools in Texas were segregated."

"What a bummer," Zooey said. "I've read about all those stupid laws, and it's hard for me to imagine not being able to have friends who are different from me. We learn so much from each other."

"I agree, Zooey. Differences can be very instructive," Edith said. "But I chose the plan my family had long dreamed for me. After medical school I accepted a residency in the main hospital in Ghana, met and married a young local doctor, went into joint practice with him in a rural area, and had three children."

Edith paused to take another sip of her drink. "I kept on working while my kids grew up and moved away. I kept working while my husband became ill and died. And then I just kept working—until I fell and broke my hip. Then, finally, I realized work was no longer all I wanted.

"So I agreed to be transported to Dallas for my replacement

surgery. My children have homes in Europe, and none of my family lives in Texas anymore. But when I was well enough to be rational, I realized that Taylor lived not too far away, so I requested to be transferred to East Texas for rehab. I was here on my own a few days, and finally I felt strong enough to ask someone to help me find her."

She took a long sip of water. "Fortunately, the name Taylor Bradford is well known around here, so it wasn't long before she and I picked up our sixty-year friendship as if we'd seen each other last week. But I was surprised to find Marilee here, too." She glanced in Marilee's direction. "I thought she was married and lived somewhere else in Texas. And I understand there's a good story waiting to be told about that."

"Whoa, hold on," Marilee said. "We're saving that story for dessert. You all know Taylor and me. And I guess we can consider this the first formal meeting of Senior Sleuths. Taylor and I decided we want to try our hands at the PI business, and you're all here to help us with our first case. Now that we all know each other, let's move on to your reports about what you've discovered at Silverado."

Edith studied some notes she had made. "As all of you must know, I'm happy in the rehab facility. I find the medical care excellent, and the staff competent and kind. But some of the residents are the victims of some awful scam in which they feel compelled to pay off so-called authorities who claim to be holding young relatives for what they call crimes. The whole thing ends up being false, a vicious extortion scheme." She lowered her voice. "A few are discussing it in the relative privacy of our beauty salon, where women have always shared personal stories. But others appear to be terrorized into silence and anxiety. And it doesn't help that the acting head administrator wants to suppress any discussion of the problem."

Zooey chimed in abruptly. "That's right. And Gloria and I have noticed that it's happening to the richest residents." She frowned. "I haven't heard anything about a resident on Medicaid being asked to pay somebody off." She made eye contact with Edith. "But the staff are saying that nothing will ever get done about these cases."

"Why not?" Marilee asked.

"Because Miss Davis, the assistant administrator who's in charge right now, won't let the police talk to any of the victims," Zooey said. "But let's don't forget our male coworker who caused a cyberscandal at the high school a few years ago. Since he works in the basement, I haven't had much contact with him. But Gloria sees him frequently."

"Yeah," Gloria said. "I was leery of him at first because I had to take him those financial disclosure forms from Miss Davis's office. I know he altered the transcripts of a couple of people who bullied him in high school, but I don't see anything sneaky about him now. He's in a position to misuse information, but he really seems to be trying to improve the information flow between Silverado and the feds. I've heard that the bills are getting paid faster since he got there."

Gloria then changed the direction of the conversation. "As for the police, they have visited Silverado a couple of times that I know of, but they never get any farther than Miss Davis, the assistant administrator temporarily in charge. I heard her tell the police they can't talk to the residents because they're disoriented and easily upset." Gloria stared at Taylor. "That might be true for Mr. Yandle, but it's certainly not true for the women. Yet Miss Davis just stops the police cold. I'm not sure how they even got enough information to decide that the criminals are in China."

"And it doesn't help that the chief of police is firmly convinced that all these types of crimes originate overseas, and that international crime is beyond the jurisdiction of his police force. Never mind that the victims are all local citizens," Taylor said, shaking her head like Gloria had.

As Taylor started to speak again, Gloria began to talk at the same time. "I don't get out around the residents as much as Zooey does, so I can't comment on what you've said about hoaxes. But from my position in the office, I suspect something else is going on, too." Her voice sounded strong. "First of all, I agree that the victims of this scam are among the wealthiest in the facility. I know this because of the financial disclosure forms I file for Miss Davis." She stopped and took a sip of water. "And something else. Miss Davis is constantly requesting the medical files on patients." She paused, and her voice weakened. "Of course, I get them for her." She paused again, for a long moment, halfway frowning, and then she said in an even stronger, firmer tone, "She may be doing something with insurance claims, but I don't exactly know what yet."

"Wow, Gloria. Good work!" Taylor said. "I hope you'll stay on this issue. If you need any help making sense of what you find, let me know. If I can't help, I'll locate someone who can."

Gloria beamed, and Zooey gave her a thumbs-up.

Taylor straightened in her chair. "So, in terms of assignments for the next few days, Gloria is staying on the paper trail in Miss Davis's office."

Gloria blushed like she'd just been named homecoming queen.

"Zooey will continue to be a good listener to find out what else we can learn about this cyberhoax dilemma," Taylor said, and Zooey raised both fists in the air as if she were the heavyweight boxing champ of the world. Gloria smiled at her. "Keep observing your former schoolmate who might have the skills to pull these scams off."

Taylor gazed at each of them steadily, then turned to Edith with a sympathetic smile. "Your job is, of course, to continue to get stronger," she said. "But when you can, we need you to keep your eyes and ears open for the same things Zooey and Gloria are monitoring. This is a mess."

Edith jotted something on the back of her agenda, which lay on the table in front of her, as if she were prescribing something for an ailing patient, then nodded once at Taylor.

"Thanks, Edith. It's so good to have you with us here at Bradford's Arbor this evening and for the duration of your stay at Silverado."

Taylor turned to Marilee. "That leaves our report. We need to catch you up on our recent brief absence. The morning this case broke wide open, Marilee and I were committed to visit Tillie Swanson, an old friend and fellow attorney who lives in Oak Cliff, part of Dallas. I had called her right after we met Shannon, our next-door-neighbor's generous friend. She listened closely when we mentioned the phone scam angle, but definitely discouraged us from working with the New Eden police chief."

"In fact, she opposed it so strongly we became suspicious," Marilee said. "I was even willing to believe she might have been involved in a scheme that financed their river cruise in France."

Taylor resumed the report. "So I called Tillie, whose daughter is the same age as Shannon and New Eden's police chief, who are also from Oak Cliff. However, Tillie isn't too well these days, so we made a date to have lunch with her at her home, which was a great idea! She told us that her daughter, the chief, and Shannon were all in high school at the same time and knew each other. He had a crush on Shannon but ended up humiliating her in front of everybody at the prom."

Once again Marilee jumped in. "If you'd been able to see the chief at work during our appointment to ask for help at Silverado, you'd know just how fond of humiliation he is."

"But," Taylor said, "Shannon had the last laugh by marrying the richest boy in the school and inheriting all his money when he died in a plane crash only a few years later. Then she used her wealth over the years to benefit residents in nursing homes in her area. In the biggest coincidence of all, Shannon and Barb—my new next-door neighbor—met at an East Texas quilt show and became good friends and traveling buddies. Marilee and I are pretty sure Shannon is supporting Barb."

"Well, I'd say that lets Shannon off the hook as our

cybercriminal, but it makes her sound like a good candidate for Senior Sleuth status—in a few years." Edith studied their small group.

"That sounds like a great idea." Taylor turned to Lois. "Will you get Shannon's contact info? We want to stay in touch with her. Lois, I know you need to slip out for your Zoom class. If we need any backup for our surveillance out at Silverado, we'll let you know." Lois nodded, and Taylor continued. "Would you tell the kitchen we're almost ready to eat?"

"Sure. I'll type these notes tomorrow morning. Anything else?"

"No. We all deserve a real meal, and then we can return to the case we're working on. Let's go to the dining room."

Once again, Edith refused to let anyone help her make the short trip.

❖

Taylor stood at the head of the table with Dr. Edith at the opposite end. The chandelier, crystal, and silver clearly awed Gloria and Zooey, and even Edith appeared to appreciate the lovely setting.

After they'd been served liberal helpings, Marilee said to the women who'd prepared and served the special meal, "Why don't you leave the platters on the table? Some of us may want second helpings." Both girls nodded vigorously, especially when Marilee mentioned the dessert that would come later.

Then, before they began to eat, Taylor picked up her glass of sparkling grape juice. "I'd like to offer a toast, to us. We're off to a fine start on our first case." She held her glass high. "I feel sure Nancy Drew would approve of our work so far." She glanced around the table. "Here's to success! And, as my granddad used to say at this point, 'Back your ears.'"

Marilee caught Gloria's confused look. "That's an old

THE NURSING HOME HOAX

Southern expression that means don't let anything come between you and your food. Enjoy!"

After they ate and drank, Edith said, "My compliments to the chef. Her chicken and vegetables are several cuts above anything we eat at Silverado." She patted her stomach, and the girls nodded. "But I don't want to lose track of *my* main reason for being here." She raised an eyebrow. "I want you to briefly fill in the gap between graduation day in 1964 and Marilee being a cohostess at Bradford's Arbor tonight." She studied each of them briefly. "I realize we have a mystery at the nursing home to solve, but I want to solve the mystery of you two first."

"Just a few more minutes, Edith," Taylor said. "Marilee has made me promise to let her tell the story, but she wants to wait till dessert. And from what I can tell, we'll be ready for that course soon."

The unusual dessert, a lemon posset popular in Britain, distracted the group for a minute, but before anyone took a bite, Edith suddenly put down her spoon. "Enough!" she said. "I've waited as long as I can. The last time I was with you two," she told Taylor and Marilee, "Taylor's commitment to practicing law in New Eden with her father had smashed your dream of a life together. Taylor did write to say that Marilee was bitterly disappointed and that she'd found somebody to marry while she was working on her master's degree. So what happened then? It was like you two had disappeared from each other's lives forever."

The girls were staring at Edith so intently they hadn't even picked up their spoons to taste their dessert, though they kept glancing at it.

"Sixty years have passed," Edith said, "and I'm back here now to find you two living at Bradford's Arbor, the same beautiful home I visited as an undergraduate. What's happened in the meantime?"

Marilee pushed her chair back from the table slightly.

"Basically, on graduation day, Taylor told me she planned to room with three other women who were going to law school." She inhaled deeply. "And that was the last time I saw her for sixty years."

"Really?" Gloria said.

"I was so stunned and disappointed at her news that I skipped our graduation ceremony, went home, and eventually married a nice man I got along well with."

"Well, how was your life? Were you ever really happy?" Zooey asked, as if seeing Marilee for the first time.

Marilee shrugged. "My husband's interests were similar to mine, and I got my MS in science, worked at a community college, traveled in the summer, and became involved in plenty of interesting professional activities both on campus and at the state level." She surveyed the small group. "I tried very hard to erase Taylor from my mind, and I was generally successful."

She was afraid she might be embarrassing Zooey and Gloria, but they appeared even more relaxed and totally focused on her story. In fact, Zooey whispered, "You go, girl!"

"And?" Edith asked. "I already know some of this story but want to be sure I'm getting it right."

Marilee absently stirred a cup of decaf she'd been served. "After my husband and I retired, we moved to Sunset Lake full-time, but his heart gave out, and he died three years ago." Her voice wavered. "I thought I would die, too, but I didn't." Both Zooey and Gloria made sympathetic noises.

"In fact, I survived and finally began to enjoy life again."

"Oh. I'm so glad," Gloria whispered so softly Marilee wondered if anyone except her heard the teenager's sympathetic words.

Marilee drew a deep breath. "Then, one day, I drove home through New Eden."

Suddenly, Taylor said, "Let's take a minute to eat our dessert. And maybe have another cup of decaf."

Edith harrumphed. "We're all just fine, and I've waited long enough to hear this next part. Marilee, please continue."

Marilee and Taylor winked at each other. "I wanted a few items," Marilee said, "so I stopped at New Eden's Piggly Wiggly grocery store. I was attracted by that unforgettable name, so I just ambled in and grabbed a cart."

She paused and addressed her small audience of four. "As I often do in unfamiliar places, I started checking my surroundings without noticing people, trying to get my bearings in the new layout. For some reason, a display of bell peppers on the produce shelves dazzled me. They were so colorful—red, green, yellow, orange. I guess I was kind of mesmerized, because suddenly I felt a jolt as my grocery cart slammed into something."

Marilee took a sip of her newly poured coffee, enjoying its smooth warmth. Then she gazed around the room. "That surprise shocked me out of my daze, and I realized I must have bumped into another customer's shopping cart." She paused. "Without looking up, I quickly began to apologize, asking whoever I'd hit if they were all right."

"Suddenly my victim began to laugh, and I almost recognized the sound. Then I saw her eyes, and...*it was Taylor*! My heart stopped and then started racing. I was laughing, but soon I was crying, too."

She stopped and gazed at Taylor, feeling almost as flushed as she had that day in the Piggly Wiggly. "That laugh had been locked in my heart for decades, and the sound of it instantly warmed and comforted me. I reached for her, not caring that our two carts were completely blocking the whole produce aisle." She felt her face turn hot. "Our hug turned into a hop, and we almost fell into the peppers—laughing, jumping, and crying."

Zooey and Gloria beamed, and Edith softly applauded.

Marilee took a deep breath. "And that's the Piggly Wiggly encounter!"

Taylor stood up. "Edith is right that we both now live here at

Bradford's Arbor. Although Marilee still owns the place at Sunset Lake, it's on the market. Just in the last month, we've gotten a little clearer about our future. We're both in our eighties, so becoming professional tennis players isn't a good plan. She's had both knees replaced, and I had a heart attack last year. Though I'm not a cardiac invalid, I am careful about diet, exercise, and stress. Being Senior Sleuths and taking on offenses against elders sounds like a perfect next step for us. And so far, the hoaxes Edith has alerted us to, and Gloria and Zooey are monitoring at Silverado, may be the perfect first case. As to our personal connection—well, that's personal. But I can say that negotiating a significant relationship between two octogenarians with a painful history is an adventure. We count on your support."

Edith picked up her dessert spoon. "Thank you two for solving the mystery of your long-delayed relationship. Now I can truly enjoy my lemon posset as much as I plan to enjoy our new enterprise of solving mysteries for other people who need our help. And you have my support."

CHAPTER IX

Professional Help

"What's our next step with Silverado's assistant administrator, Miss Davis? The one that everybody talked about at dinner last night," Marilee asked.

Taylor huffed, then shrugged. "What would you say to sitting down to talk?"

Marilee stopped, holding Taylor's arm to steady herself as she reached down to work a pebble out of her right sandal. "Whew. That's better. That rock was distracting me. And yes, I'd like to give my knees a rest. There's a bench just up there."

Taylor groaned slightly as she sat. "You know the main reason I haven't taken down my shingle yet? Somehow the fact that I'm still a licensed attorney makes people realize I haven't gone completely gaga."

"Aha. So that's why you just paid for another year of upkeep on the Bradford and Bradford website. Thanks for the insight." Marilee rubbed her right knee. "What about Miss Davis? To me she sounds hostile and secretive," Marilee said.

"But those traits are hardly illegal."

"Maybe Zooey is on to something when she says that Miss Davis gets fidgety if she talks to the residents very much. And Gloria, when she observes that Miss Davis acts nervous about her work, like she's afraid Gloria will uncover something."

"Yes. And accusing Edith of spreading rumors is even worse. That's the last thing Edith would ever do."

Marilee turned to face Taylor. "I propose that we get to know Miss Davis a little better. Were you able to make an appointment to talk with her yet?"

"I'm glad you brought up this subject because yes, I have a meeting scheduled for tomorrow afternoon. In preparation, I asked Lois to do a little research. She discovered that our Miss Davis has been rather active in small claims court over the years and has won several cases, which all involve money judgments in her favor."

"Really? How much money, Taylor?"

"Nothing huge, but maybe she's more interested in her bank account than in other people."

"How sad," Marilee said. "I hate to envision someone like that working at a nursing home. The residents there deserve to be surrounded by kind, loving, generous people, not someone who sounds as grasping as Miss Davis does."

"I hear you, Marilee. But Miss Davis isn't the only worry. There's also the girls' schoolmate. What's his name?"

"It's John Gamble, I think, but if Lois is this good at research, we ought to ask her to have a go at his background, too. I'll text Zooey and ask her to send any relevant info about him to Lois. Sound good?"

"Sure. What else before we start the long trek back home?"

"Well, do you want to say anything more about not being gaga yet? Frankly, I'm amazed at what a great time we've been having since we decided to become the Senior Sleuths. I feel like it's helped give me some focus and the possibility of fun even as an octogenarian. How about you?"

"For me, it's like slipping into a new gear. Since we've gotten a clear idea of the type of client we want to work for, I feel much less pressure to constantly take on new cases. I'm aware of a kind of professional excitement I haven't felt for a while. I even have slightly more energy, though I still huff and puff when I get to the top of the stairs."

"Now, Taylor. You can't complain about a little shortness of breath. Not after the heart attack you've had. But that's why we're being good about our evening walks. It's part of our movement and exercise plan."

"Of course, you're right. And I want to add one more thing. I'm beginning to believe I can live with the bargain we've made about our personal relationship. At first, I thought I couldn't tolerate living together without being able to act on my passion for you. But you've made your feelings for me clear: admiration, respect, and love. Hugs and kisses only. That doesn't fit my personal definition of romance, but given that clarity about your boundaries, I can respect them. Who knows? Maybe we're creating a new form of romance. On that note, how about we start back home? After a hug, of course. And a little kiss."

Bright and early Monday morning, at the breakfast table, Marilee turned to Taylor, who sat reading her morning paper, New Eden being one of the few smaller towns in East Texas that had managed to keep its local newspaper. "Let me interrupt for a minute to ask if you've had any further thoughts about involving some form of law enforcement in this case. I take the point that our local chief won't help, but shouldn't we let someone know what's going on?"

"I've been thinking along the same lines. Why don't I call a friend who's been on a task force in Dallas concerned with elder abuse? Maybe she'd have some suggestions."

Marilee pushed Taylor's cell phone closer.

"Why not right now? I'll bet she's already in the office. Give her a call."

Taylor folded the paper and put it aside. She picked up the

cell and located the number. The next thing Marilee heard was Taylor's warm greeting.

"Howdy, friend. What's up with you?"

Marilee followed Taylor's half of the conversation intently. Taylor's friend responded briefly and then apparently asked how Taylor had been. Not one to dally on the phone, Taylor quickly stated the reason for her call. "My friend Marilee Connor and I are trying to help people our age avoid being taken advantage of financially, and we think some of that is going on at one of our local nursing homes. Several residents have been asked to pay significant sums to help a younger relative avoid arrest or physical harm because of an imaginary infraction. Know anything about situations like that?"

Marilee couldn't hear the response, but Taylor was soon talking again. "Yes, this is occurring in my East Texas town, New Eden. And we *have* talked with our chief of police, who's aware of the situation but convinced that the criminals are in China and his hands are tied in dealing with international crime. The poor sod also believes the Texas Rangers are the ones who have the mandate to deal with cell phone and cybercrime. So, we need your expertise. Who can we inform about the situation so someone will know what's going on in case we need backup?"

Marilee offered a quick arm-pump to encourage Taylor's efforts.

"You say you've heard of a federal task force with an undercover member right here in New Eden? Fantastic! How can I reach that person? The assistant administrator at the nursing home has essentially refused to let the local police talk with any residents, so I doubt our case is even on the record here. I'd really like to talk with the undercover officer to learn more about what's going on."

Taylor gestured for the pencil with which Marilee had begun to fill in the newspaper's crossword puzzle and grabbed the newspaper to write on. "Go ahead. I'm ready to copy, and I promise to burn the paper afterward." After jotting down a name and number, Taylor quickly ended the phone call. "Thanks so much, friend. I really appreciate your help. Talk with you soon, I hope."

"Well, that sounded productive," Marilee said.

"I hope you're right. I got the name and number of a local police sergeant who's working undercover with an FBI task force on elder abuse. My friend doesn't know her well but has heard good things about her and terrible things about our police chief. So, why don't I get out of my pajamas and into the Senior Sleuths' office and see what she has to say?"

"Perfect, and I'll get dressed, too. But at least tell me the name of this new contact. I'm hoping she'll make a big difference for the folks at Silverado."

"Well, yes. But my buddy asked me to let this undercover officer call the shots on how involved she gets. The Elder Abuse Task Force may well be focused on other crimes and suspects, so we'll need to be sensitive to her situation. Her name is Elise Mora, and I'll be glad to catch you up on what she says as soon as you can get dressed and into the office."

"Are you saying I'll be that much slower than you?"

"Yes, exactly. This isn't the right time for a speakerphone conversation, so plan to catch up afterward. And don't hurry. I know that dressing is a mysteriously time-consuming process for you." With that, Taylor dropped her napkin onto her plate, grabbed her cell phone, and raced out of the room.

Marilee picked up the breakfast dishes and headed for the sink.

CHAPTER X

A New Suspect

"I'm glad you decided to come with me, Marilee. I feel like I'm about to question a hostile witness, which isn't one of my best things." Taylor pushed the metal bar that opened one of the two heavy glass-paned doors at the front of Silverado, then held it while Marilee walked in after her.

"Feel like you could use a little backup, eh?" Marilee peeked down the long hall that led to the dining room. "I'm not entirely oriented to this building yet, but it obviously has a typical layout. On each side, there's a long corridor, with a room every twenty feet or so. How many senior citizens does it accommodate?"

Taylor glanced around the facility as if she'd never set foot in it before. "You know, I've never asked. My dad stayed in a small suite on that hall to our left, and when I came to visit, I walked straight to his room without stopping, except at the small table where someone was usually working on a jigsaw puzzle. A lot of times we ate in the dining room, which is that large, blue-walled area straight ahead of us, with a grand piano and a large bookcase. But I never explored the other wing. I assume it's similar, though who knows?" Taylor frowned. "I don't recall ever seeing the assistant administrator when I visited Dad, though I did hear some of the staff refer to Miss Davis and assumed that was her name. No one ever called her by her first name. Most of my dealings were with the chief administrator, who's out on leave."

"What do you imagine our Miss Davis looks like?" Marilee whispered, though the hall was empty.

"I have no idea. I never even saw her office door open. Could have been a giant octopus in there, and I wouldn't have known."

"Come on. Surely she made an appearance occasionally. According to the girls and to Edith, she emerges often enough to make threatening remarks to them. And she has to be out and about to observe their interactions with the residents."

Taylor shrugged. "Maybe she keeps a low profile with the general public and leaves her office only in off hours. I'm glad I called ahead for an appointment. We might not be able to talk to her if I hadn't."

Marilee elbowed Taylor and pointed out the office door to their right. "Well, that must be where she does her thing." The door was closed, the black-and-white sign reading *MISS DAVIS, Assistant Administrator* amended with a piece of paper partially covering the word *Assistant*. The paper had the word *Acting* handwritten on it. "Rather stark contrast to the chief administrator's cute nameplate adorned with metal daisies, isn't it?" Marilee asked.

"Huh. I never noticed until you pointed it out," Taylor said. "But Miss Davis's sign gives me the feeling she won't welcome our visit nearly as much as the administrator of Silverado would have."

Marilee squeezed Taylor's forearm. "We'll see," she said. "Miss Davis may turn out to simply be shy or really matter-of-fact."

"Or not."

"Well, we'll never find out if we don't let her know we're here for our two o'clock appointment. I'm guessing she wouldn't be happy if we were tardy."

"You're probably right." Taylor knocked, and the door

opened so abruptly, she was afraid she'd fall into the office when a frail, small woman appeared.

"Hello," she said. "How can I help you?"

"We have an appointment with Miss Davis."

"An appointment?" The woman shook her head as if she didn't know the meaning of the word.

"I'm Taylor Bradford, and this is my associate Marilee Connor. I'm a local lawyer and would like to consult Miss Davis about some events that have recently occurred at Silverado."

"Bradford, Bradford," the woman murmured, rummaging around on her cluttered desk and finally locating what appeared to be an appointment book. She opened it and ran her finger down a pristine page. "Oh, yes. Here's your name. It had slipped my mind that Miss Davis is scheduled to see you. It's unusual for her to allow anyone to interrupt her here at work."

Taylor elbowed Marilee, who raised an eyebrow.

"Miss Davis will see you now," the woman said, peering at the hall behind them as if a long line of people might be there trying to see her boss.

The secretary was younger than Taylor and Marilee, but the years had not been kind. She hunched over, causing her to appear pained as she crept toward the door behind her desk. It, too, had a piece of paper correcting *Assistant* for *Acting Administrator*.

Taylor had to force herself to wait while the worn-looking secretary inched toward the closed door, every step measured and deliberate. Finally, the woman tapped gently on it and almost whispered. "Your two o'clock appointment is here, Miss Davis."

An answer bayoneted the air of the outer office. "All right. I'm very busy, so I'll need to get this over with as quickly as possible."

The secretary winced, twisted the knob of the office door, and slowly waved Taylor and Marilee into the starkest space Taylor had ever witnessed. The gray walls were bare except for the numerous filing cabinets that lined them like Prussian soldiers. The dull surface of Miss Davis's metal desk held only a silver laptop, and, behind it, a woman glared at them.

"Well, state your business." Miss Davis glanced up from her computer. "I have many demands on my time." She glanced back at her screen as if apologizing to it for the interruption. Her secretary winced and turned to creep out the door, giving Marilee a sympathetic nod as she closed it softly behind her.

Marilee gazed around, probably for somewhere to sit, but then shrugged and just stood there beside Taylor, waiting for her to state her case.

"I realize you're busy, Miss Davis," Taylor said.

Miss Davis scowled. "I am. So will you please get to the point. I don't have time for any pleasantries."

Taylor shifted from one foot to the other, uncharacteristically at a loss for words.

Miss Davis sniffed impatiently "Please state the reason for your visit. I don't have much time, especially now that I'm having to assume the director's duties while she's out on sick leave."

"Of course. You don't know me, though maybe you do know that I've been a lawyer here in New Eden for almost sixty years. Perhaps you've heard of Bradford and Bradford?"

Miss Davis shrugged. "Perhaps. I rarely consult a lawyer. I can almost always represent myself effectively. That way I don't waste money." She paused, then continued as if weighing every word she uttered. "I don't want to sound disagreeable, but most people are weak and gullible. They're the ones that need the services you and your kind offer."

Taylor noticed Marilee roll her eyes when Miss Davis stared at her computer screen again and typed something.

"I understand your position and respect your independent spirit." Taylor took a deep breath. "But as one professional to another, I'd appreciate your opinion about some rather suspicious events here at Silverado that we have been made aware of."

Miss Davis tore her eyes away from her computer screen. "And what suspicious events might you be referring to?"

Taylor cleared her throat. "I'm certain that a woman in your position in this facility would know about the well-being of each resident here."

Miss Davis inclined her head slightly, clearly expecting Taylor to continue.

"It has come to my attention that one of the women here, a Mrs. Gray, has been forced to pay a large amount of money to someone who falsely claimed to be representing her grandson."

Miss Davis scowled. "Ah. That woman clearly needs stronger medication. I have no doubt that she's blown her story all out of proportion. It's a mistake to take seriously the stories these old women concoct. They don't have anything else to do, so they fabricate elaborate fantasies to while away the time. That's why I usually keep my office door closed. Otherwise, I'd never get any work done. They'd all be pouring in and bothering me with their sob stories. Furthermore, they gossip about all this nonsense to other residents, spreading fear and distrust. I've even had to limit visits from the police. They just make the delusions worse."

Marilee hadn't said a word since they'd been ushered into this barren environment, but suddenly she spoke in a tight, angry tone that immediately drew Taylor's attention. "I've recently heard several stories like Mrs. Gray's here in this facility, and the women sound rational and convincing. They, and at least one man, are clearly being victimized, and it's up to you, as the temporary chief administrator, to intervene."

Miss Davis glared at her. "As if I don't have anything else to do but deal with baseless rumors our clientele dream up. My plate is full to overflowing. And you are…? Were we introduced?"

Marilee stood even taller than usual, her almost-six-foot height impressive. "I'm a retired college professor, and I know defensive subterfuge when I hear it. These residents pay good money to stay here, and you are legally obligated to protect them from predators." She turned and stalked to the door. "I've heard all the defensive gobbledygook I can take for one day. I'll wait for you out in the hall, Taylor."

Miss Davis grimaced as Marilee strode out of the office. "Academics. In my experience, most college professors can't tell an invoice from a debit card. I'd hate to have someone like her taking care of my well-being."

Taylor had to force herself not to follow Marilee's lead out the door. "Since you're obviously an expert in the area of wellness, shouldn't it be your job to investigate the emotionally and financially distressing experiences your residents are having?"

Taylor expected no reply, so she prepared to leave. But just then Miss Davis's secretary reentered the room, leading a little Pomeranian on an obviously expensive leash. Miss Davis suddenly acted like she'd just been granted an audience with Warren Buffett.

"Hello there, my little angel. Does it want Mommy to take it for a little walkie-walk? I'll be ready before you know it. My visitor was just going." She opened the top drawer of her desk and pulled out an expensively packaged bag of treats. "Come on over here, sweetie cakes. I've got something special for you, my little lamb."

Taylor followed the secretary out. Clearly, if she'd said anything, Miss Davis wouldn't have heard it.

❖

Marilee stood near the entrance, staring through the glass door toward the street and tapping her right foot as if she were playing drums in a jazz band. Obviously, she was waiting for Taylor.

When Taylor touched her, she whirled around as if ready to pull a handgun out of her purse. Luckily, she didn't own a weapon.

"Well, that was a useless trip," Marilee said. "At least now I can sympathize with Zooey and Gloria. Can you imagine having to work for that woman? Her secretary shows the results of reporting to her directly. What a piece of work Miss Davis is. I wouldn't put anything past her."

Taylor took her hand and led her to a quiet part of the entry area. "I agree, though after you left, I did manage to discover her soft spot."

"I don't believe you. That woman's made of solid brass. She doesn't have a weak spot anywhere."

"Let's sit here for a minute and recuperate. I feel like I've played three sets of tennis in the summer heat, which I haven't done since I was in my thirties." They sat side by side on a convenient couch and remained silent for several minutes. Then, finally, after Marilee quit tapping her foot ninety to nothing, Taylor spoke. "I'd have to agree with you a hundred percent if I hadn't seen her other side."

"Other side?" Marilee started tapping her foot again. "That woman doesn't have another side. She's one-dimensional, and that dimension is rigid and unyielding."

"But you didn't see the cute little dog that made her rush me out of her office so she could give it some expensive treats and take it outside for a little *walkie-walk*."

"I don't believe you."

"Believe me. But that's beside the point. She'll obviously never help us find out who's cheating these poor old people out of their life's savings."

"That's for sure. She's greedy through and through. Did you see the way she inspected us—our clothes, our jewelry?"

"No. Not really."

"Well, I did. It was like she could tell where we bought everything we wore, how long we'd had it, and how much we paid for it."

"How did you come up with that observation?"

Marilee cocked her head to one side. "I do have a few secrets you haven't discovered yet, though they're all pleasant ones. But as to how, I had an aunt who could size up somebody's bank account after she glanced at their shoes."

"Really?"

"Yep. It was almost like she was psychic. And she did have a gift," Marilee said. "But she put her talent to good use."

"How was that?"

"Oh, people would come to her with their personal problems, and she could, and would, almost always help them figure out what was wrong and how they could make life better for themselves."

"Did she study psychology in college?"

"No. But she did get her GED years after she ran away and got married when she was a sophomore in high school."

"So it really was a gift."

"Yes. She should have been a therapist. She was a great listener and had a lot of compassion for everyone she met and talked to. She could really help people with their personal problems, and she loved doing it."

"The exact opposite of Miss Davis, I suppose." Taylor took Marilee's hand and squeezed it as they leaned back on the couch and shared a comfortable silence.

After several minutes, Marilee said quietly, "You know, it's sad."

Taylor turned to her. "What's sad?"

"Something tells me that Miss Davis has the same type of gift my aunt had, but she's chosen to use it exclusively for her own benefit instead of for the good of others."

After a long silence, Taylor said, "That *is* sad. Especially for these poor seniors here who are being abused and cut off from help."

Marilee turned to her with mischief in her eyes. "How bad would it be to stop at Chat n Chew for a single-dip fudge sundae on the way home? I could use some chocolate therapy."

CHAPTER XI

Tailing a Suspect

"Our dinner with Edith and the girls went well the other night, didn't it?" Taylor asked as she and Marilee sat side by side in their front-porch swing, catching a rare wisp of cool air as they recovered from their evening walk.

"It was excellent. But what are we going to do about that perfectly horrid Miss Davis?"

Taylor took a deep breath. "I was hoping you wouldn't bring her up, but you're right. She's definitely my chief suspect in this nursing home hoax."

Taylor planted her feet on their wooden front porch and pushed the swing into action.

"Whoa. Why'd you do that?" Marilee grabbed the metal chain that held up each end of the swing.

"We need to get moving on this case." Taylor planted her feet on the porch and got out of the swing. "Come on."

"Where are you going?"

"To call the girls, and I left my phone in the house." She took a few steps, then turned back to Marilee, who hadn't budged. "We need to know more about our Miss Davis and what she gets up to when she's not closed up in her office at Silverado. But we're probably not the ones to shadow her."

"Yes." Marilee moved slowly, fanning herself as she rose

and then caught up with Taylor. "You're right about that woman. She'd spot us immediately." She took Taylor's hand and squeezed it. "But won't she make a connection between us and the girls?"

Taylor stopped. She and Marilee had to do something constructive about the situation at Silverado. "She probably has never seen us talking to the girls out there, as seldom as she gets out of her office during visiting hours. And neither of us directly recommended them. They applied for the jobs on their own and made their own deals with Mrs. Hurd before her leave started." She shrugged. "Anyway, it's worth a shot. We haven't made much progress, and we need to before another incident occurs. Let's call the junior sleuths."

❖

"Hi, Zooey. How's it going out at Silverado? Are you and Gloria doing okay?" Taylor sat at her desk in her office, waving to Marilee as she talked into her cell phone. "Hey. I know this is asking a lot, Zooey, but could you and Gloria arrange your work schedules out at Silverado so you can keep an eye on Miss Davis after she leaves the facility?" Taylor asked. "I understand you'd rather stay as far away from her as you can, but we're afraid she's up to no good. Marilee's here. I'll put you on speaker."

"She's the most awful woman I've ever known," Zooey said. "I can't stand the thought of being anywhere near her."

Marilee nodded vigorously.

Taylor glanced at her and winked.

Just then Gloria chimed in on Zooey's phone. "I don't like the woman either, so I'd enjoy seeing her get what she deserves."

"Gloria," Zooey said. "I can't believe my ears. I've never heard you say anything bad about anybody."

Taylor and Marilee studied each other, and each covered her mouth to keep from laughing out loud, Marilee's eyes almost tearing up.

"I can't help it, Zooey," Gloria said. "She *is* a disgusting woman. And I'll gladly do whatever I can to see if she's the one being so cruel to these poor old people out here. Taking their money like that is a real crime."

"So you'd be willing to follow her," Taylor said.

"Well, I guess we'll have to, especially since Gloria is gung-ho." Zooey paused. "You know, I've always wanted to be a spy. All those movies on TV make it so exciting. Now Gloria and I'll get to see what it's like in real life. Hey, Glo," she said. "Isn't that right?"

"Yeah. It'll be fun. But I don't guess we'll need to wear disguises, will we, Zooey?"

Taylor spoke up. "No. You definitely won't need to wear disguises because you must not let her see you. We just need to know where she goes and who she sees. Now that you mention it, maybe I better call your mothers to let them know what we're asking you to do."

"Oh, you don't need to do that. We're legally adults. Our moms know we're doing some undercover work for you, and they've talked with each other about it. They're cool. But talking about tailing people might make them nervous. We'll be very careful as we find out what the horrible Miss Davis is up to." She lowered her voice. "Tay and Mare, we'll keep in touch. Zooey and Gloria, junior sleuths, over and out."

"Bye, y'all," Gloria said right before Zooey clicked off her phone.

Taylor and Marilee both beamed, then gave each other a high-five. "Well, Tay," Marilee said. "Sounds like we've got enthusiastic junior partners."

"And it feels pretty good, doesn't it, Mare?"

"But I hate that nickname. It makes me sound like a horse, and I'm not happy about the comparison."

"Understood. I'll never say it again, and I'll let the girls know how you feel."

❖

The next night, Taylor and Marilee had just finished their second game of Scrabble when Taylor's cell sounded. "It's kind of late for a call, isn't it?" she murmured and checked her phone. "It's Zooey," she told Marilee. "Do you think she and Gloria have already had some luck with their new mission?"

"Hey, Tay," Zooey said softly.

"Zooey. What's going on?" Taylor switched to speakerphone and nodded to Marilee, hoping the girls weren't already having problems.

"Glo and I hung around the Silverado parking lot a little while ago and saw Miss Davis leave. So we hopped into my van and followed her. She has a brand-new Cadillac and a big house in a swanky neighborhood. I was surprised."

"It's possible she has extra sources of income beyond her salary at Silverado," Taylor said.

"Well, she obviously spends money on her dog, her car, and her home. That must add up," Zooey said.

Gloria joined the conversation. "We had to sit out in Zo's car, a couple of houses down from Miss Davis's home, and almost burned up. I was sweating all over. Ew. But it was either that or use all Zo's gas on air conditioning. I told her she should have filled up yesterday."

Marilee rolled her eyes, and Taylor said, "We need to give you two a gas allowance for this mission, don't we?"

Marilee silently clapped, and both girls softly cheered, "Yeah. Great idea."

"Okay. Now that's taken care of, what else did you find out, besides where she lives?" Taylor asked.

"Well, it's very obvious that she's crazy about that little mutt of hers," Zooey said.

Taylor raised an eyebrow. "Why do you say that?"

"Because she let it in and out of the house about a million

times while we were sitting out there sweating to beat the band. And she never let it out of her sight. I'm surprised she hasn't bought it a solid-gold collar and a little air-conditioned sports car to drive around in."

"Yeah. I wish she'd treat Silverado residents more like she treats that dog," Gloria said.

"You've got that right," Zooey added.

"Focus, you two. You're on a mission," Taylor said, winking at Marilee. "We need you to keep your eyes peeled and to be as invisible as possible. In fact—"

"Whoa, Tay. Miss Davis just got in her car and is backing out of her driveway. Duck, Glo. We can't afford to let her see us. Over and out to headquarters."

"Well, at least they're taking their mission somewhat seriously." Taylor took a deep breath. "I can't wait to learn where she goes."

❖

"I'm getting worried about the girls," Marilee told Taylor. "It's been at least two hours since we talked to them. I thought we'd hear right back."

"Oh, you know how kids are. They probably decided to stop by the Dairy Queen and ran into a bunch of their friends. Most likely they're cutting up with them right now and have forgotten all about their Miss Davis mission."

"Yeah." Marilee stood in front of the bathroom mirror, anointing her face with her age-defying night cream. "Miss Davis was probably heading to Piggly Wiggly to stock up on dog food. I bet she feeds that little mutt the most expensive brand available."

"Well, at least she cares about something. I like it that she has some kind of soft spot." Taylor started flossing her teeth.

"You're right. Having a soft spot for something, or someone, is a point in that person's favor, isn't it?"

"I agree." Taylor's phone suddenly squawked, and she

whirled around, rushing into the sitting room to put it on mute. "Damn Amber Alert. I know their messages are important, but it's late—" She stopped and suddenly turned. "Marilee, did you hear my phone go off earlier?"

Marilee strolled from the bathroom into the second-floor sitting room, where Taylor was staring at her phone. "No. Why? We did both take a shower, but one of us should have heard it."

"Huh. This call was from Zooey, and she's already left several messages, the first one about an hour ago. Let me pull it up and read it to you."

We're following Miss Davis, and she's heading toward town. We're staying a long way behind her, but from what we can tell, she's heading toward the downtown business area. Talk to you later.

Marilee brushed her hair more forcefully than usual. "What does the next one say?"

Taylor scrolled down. "Here it is. From Zooey again."

Miss Davis just turned into the parking lot at the city hall. Now she's getting out of her car and heading toward the building.

"Who in the world could she be going to see?" Marilee said. "Here's a wild idea. Maybe she's having an affair with a man that works there." She laughed.

"You're right. That's a wild idea. But here's another message, and then another. I can't believe we missed all these. Maybe if we hadn't gone downstairs to get you some ice cream—"

"It doesn't matter now, Taylor," Marilee said. "No need to beat me up. We didn't have any idea they'd discover something this soon. What does the next message say?"

Miss Davis is walking into the city hall, and we're sneaking in right behind her. Caught the door just in time, but it was close.

"Uh. Those girls are taking more risks than I like. I hope they don't get into trouble. Maybe we shouldn't have—"

The phone dinged, and Taylor answered it immediately. "Hey, Zooey. I'm sorry we didn't pick up. What's going on?'

"We've been creeping down the corridor on the second floor of the city hall, following Miss Davis." Zooey was talking so fast she was running some of her words together. "We just passed the door to the city manager's office and are watching where Miss Davis is going." Zooey was whispering now. "Hey. It's the assistant city manager's office. Why would she be sneaking in there at this time of night?"

"Like I said earlier, maybe they're having an affair," Marilee whispered to Taylor, who held up one finger in a just-a-minute gesture.

"She walked right in and left the door cracked, so we're peeking in," Zooey said. "She's taking a bunch of papers out of her briefcase and handing them to him—"

Zooey's phone banged like she'd dropped it.

"What are you two doing here?" It was a man's voice. "I'll have to ask you to leave immediately. How did you get in here? These offices closed hours ago."

And then the phone went dead.

❖

"My god, Taylor. What should we do?" Marilee jumped up. "We have to help those girls."

Taylor immediately punched a string of numbers into her phone. "Don't worry. When I talked with her, Sergeant Mora gave me her numbers at work and at home as well as the hours she's on duty. She's working tonight. I'm calling to explain the situation. Maybe she can keep our girls from being booked."

After a brief conversation, Taylor turned to Marilee. "Fortune is smiling on us. Elise just learned that a man who works for the assistant city manager intercepted the girls. Just by luck he'd stayed late in the office, but here's the amazing part. That guy is also a member of the task force Elise is on. He didn't want his boss and Miss Davis to know they were being watched, so he intercepted the girls before they could be discovered. Then he got them out of the building with neither his boss nor Miss Davis any the wiser."

"Thank goodness." Marilee sat back down. "I was scared to death that something bad had happened to those two. I'd never be able to live with myself—"

Taylor sat beside her and put an arm around her. "Those girls probably won't stop talking about this big adventure for a long time, even though they may be upset right now. What if we text them and invite them to come for breakfast in the morning? It's too late to debrief tonight, but tomorrow would be good."

Marilee suddenly sat up. "What if we're on the wrong track entirely? You and I don't have any evidence that Miss Davis has done anything illegal, and we don't know much about the assistant city manager. I wouldn't know him if he walked into the room right now."

"You're right. Of course, I know him by sight, but I haven't had much to do with him." Taylor stood up, kicked off her shoes, and raised one foot so she could rub a sore spot under her big toe.

Marilee gazed at her. "I wish I could stand on one foot like that. You're pretty agile for a woman of advanced age."

Taylor shrugged. "Thanks. I like to exercise. But back to the assistant city manager. I've heard he's lived here all his life, is in his late forties, and is rather handsome, with an eye for the ladies. But let's do one thing at a time. I'll text the girls about meeting in the morning, and maybe Elise will have time to join us somewhere for lunch. We need to do some catching up with her, too. Sleep well, podner."

CHAPTER XII

A Pair of Reports

"Hey, Tay. Come let us in!"

"What the..." Taylor rubbed her eyes and rolled out of bed to go look out her window.

"It's the girls," Marilee said as she emerged from her room next door, carrying the feather pillow she'd just removed from over her head. "What time is it? The sun's barely up."

Taylor glanced at the digital clock on a nearby antique chest of drawers. "A little before six. What are they doing here? Especially this early."

"Heaven only knows. But we better let them in before they wake up the neighborhood." Marilee yawned and pulled on the lightweight pink housecoat she'd grabbed, along with her pillow, on her way to Taylor's room. "Oh. I could use about four more hours' sleep."

"I wish I had their energy, but we did invite them for breakfast," Taylor said. "I had no idea this was their idea of breakfast time." She walked over to one of the bedroom windows and raised it. "Girls. Be quiet," she called. "I'll let you in in a few minutes."

"Okay, Tay," Zooey yelled. "But hurry. We've got a lot to tell you."

Taylor brushed her short white hair back, still wearing her favorite shortie pajamas.

"Tay!"

"We better get down there soon, or Zooey will wake up the entire town," Marilee said.

Taylor walked back to the window, waved at the girls, and then gave them a thumbs-up. "I can't believe they're not phoning us instead of yelling like this."

Marilee toed her feet into a pair of old tennis shoes she used for walking. "They must really be stirred up. Let's go."

❖

Suddenly, the front doorbell rang, several times in a row. "I'll let them in," Marilee said, "before they take a battering ram to the door."

"Right. Nothing shy about those girls."

"Hey, Tay," Zooey called as she bolted through the door Marilee had just opened a crack. "Wait till you hear about our night."

"Come into the kitchen, you two," Marilee said.

"This is a little earlier than we usually have breakfast, but it won't take long to get something on the table," Taylor said. The girls trailed them into the kitchen and stood around while she pulled out some fresh sweet rolls she'd picked up at the bakery the day before.

"I'm so excited, I don't think I can eat anything this early," Zooey said. "What about you, Glo?"

Gloria shook her head hesitantly.

"Sure I can't get you something?" Marilee started the coffee machine, which began filling the kitchen with a rich, full aroma.

"Well, just a little cup of coffee. And maybe one of those rolls? Glo and I could split one."

"Huh," Gloria said. "I bet there's enough for me to have my own."

They all laughed. "Sounds like last night's adventure gave Gloria an appetite after all." Marilee glanced at Gloria. "How do you take your coffee?"

"A lot of sugar and cream, Miss Marilee." She pulled back, suddenly solemn.

"It's okay, Gloria. Marilee and I want you to feel at home here, so don't hesitate to just be yourself," Taylor said.

Gloria sat down at the breakfast table. "Thank you. Last night was really strange, and I still kinda feel like I'm dreaming."

"Ah, Lee. It was strange, but Glo and I took care of everything just fine." Then Zooey said to Marilee, "Taylor told us you didn't like Mare as a nickname, so I'm switching to Lee. How's that?"

"Tons better. Thanks." Marilee squeezed Zooey's arm gently.

Taylor placed some saucers, forks, sweet rolls, and a large plate of fruit on the kitchen table and motioned for Zooey and Gloria to sit. "We need to catch up. Elise Mora, our contact at the New Eden police, told us that you'd been discovered by a man who supposedly works for the assistant city manager. But he's really observing him for the Elder Abuse Task Force that Sergeant Mora herself is on. Do you girls feel like telling us what happened after your phone went dead last night?"

Zooey was focusing on the rolls and Gloria on the fruit, but Zooey finally replied. "Well, the guy hustled us out of the building so fast it made us dizzy. He showed us the front door and told us to go home. And we got out of there, fast."

"Go back to before you got thrown out. What about the man Miss Davis was visiting? Did you hear what they were discussing?"

"No. Not really. They were in his office, which said Assistant City Manager on the door, not talking very loud, but I did hear Miss Davis say, 'We need to be really careful. I can't afford to have any trouble.'"

Taylor cleared her throat. "I know you two are old enough to know that married adults sometimes cheat on their spouses. While Miss Davis is insistently 'Miss,' the guy might well be married. They could be having an affair they don't want folks to know about."

Gloria reddened, and Zooey tossed her head to one side. "Of course. Could that be it, Glo?"

"Uh. Maybe."

"As a lawyer who has handled my fair share of divorces," Taylor said, "I unfortunately know how often married people stray."

"Whatever's going on, the guy that threw us out really didn't want us to see anything. And he sure didn't want those two to see us." Zooey sighed. "But it would have made a great story to tell about riding in the squad car and being afraid they might throw me into a dirty old jail cell and not give me anything but bread and water to eat and—"

"Okay, Zooey. That's enough. Don't get carried away," Taylor said. "You know that's not what happened."

Zooey scrunched up her face. "But it's so much more interesting than the truth."

Marilee poured everyone a fresh cup of coffee, then sat. "And what is the truth? Zooey? Gloria?"

Zooey grabbed another roll and took a bite. "Oh, all right."

"Well, now that we know you've been thrown out of city hall," Taylor said, "what was the next chapter of your saga of last night?"

Zooey picked up their story. "We were way too jazzed to just go home to bed, but the DQ was already closed, so we just drove over to my house and replayed the whole scene."

The girls smiled at each other. "In fact, we imagined how it could have gone down from several different angles," Gloria said.

"I get the picture. You haven't slept at all, have you?" Marilee asked.

"That's exactly right," Zooey said.

"We don't have much to add, but we're meeting with Elise later," Taylor explained. "She may be able to add a few details. She and the guy who caught you two are on a task force investigating elder crime. And the assistant city manager oversees city-owned nursing homes, of which Silverado is one. The undercover officer must be trying to get information about the city's involvement in the nursing home business. We'll know more later today. Right now, you two get some sleep. How'd you get here? I didn't see Zooey's van."

"To be honest, we walked. We couldn't go to sleep, so we just started out and finally ended up here. But it was earlier than we thought," Zooey said.

Taylor jumped up. "Just let me get Marilee's keys and take you both where you need to go. After the night you've had, you deserve some free taxi service."

"Good idea," Marilee said. "I didn't get all the beauty sleep I needed last night either, so you'll know where to find me when you get back."

"Which will be sooner rather than later," Taylor said. "Come on, girls. We all need some rest."

❖

Taylor whispered, "Wake up, sleepyhead. I've had my shower. It's getting close to lunchtime, so you need to start getting ready for our meeting with Elise. I'd like to hear her side of the story about last night's activities."

Marilee stretched and yawned. "I still feel like I've been rode hard and put away wet."

Taylor chuckled. "I haven't heard that old expression in forever. And I know what you mean. But crooks never take a holiday, so we need to find out the latest from Elise."

"Oh, okay." Marilee got up, showered, and put on a lightweight turquoise blouse and a pair of white slacks, then stuck her head into Taylor's room. "I'll be ready as soon as I finish my makeup. How about we meet her out at the Whataburger? I'm in the mood for one of their chicken sandwiches."

Taylor pushed back her white hair, damp from her shower, and took her time pulling on an orange cotton shirt with some black capri pants. She hadn't had a court date to attend in several weeks and was happy with her semi-retired life. Lately, she'd been able to dress a lot more comfortably than the frequent times during her career she'd had to wear a suit and heels all day. She picked up her phone and located Elise's contact number.

She and Marilee rendezvoused in the upstairs sitting room, ready for another day of hunting criminals. "Okay. Elise told me she'd meet us at the Whataburger in half an hour, so we can take our time."

When they drove up to the burger joint, Taylor spotted Elise at the front counter, obviously waiting to order.

"Do you want the usual?" Taylor asked Marilee as they started to get out of the car. Marilee, probably groggy from her interrupted sleep, hadn't even complained when Taylor drove them to the Whataburger in her little sports car. In fact, Taylor almost missed Marilee's moaning, groaning, and snide remarks about her vehicle and fast driving.

"That's right. And a free senior drink. A large iced tea."

"You can afford to pay for your drink, Marilee," Taylor said.

"But why should I? It's free, and we're definitely seniors."

Taylor shrugged. She'd learned to overlook most of Marilee's penny-pinching ways. Almost.

"I'll get us a booth or a table, whichever's the most private," Marilee said. "I'm sure what we talk about will be hush-hush."

"Of course," Taylor said, and they went in different directions after they pushed through the heavy glass door into the frigid air-conditioned entry.

"I see you beat us," Taylor said to Elise as she walked up behind her in the line of waiting customers.

"Not by much. How's it going?"

"Fine. It's pretty quiet at the office right now. What about you?"

"Really busy, especially after last night."

"Sorry about—"

"Don't worry about it. It gave us a great break from the same old same old."

"Our junior sleuths are having a great time. Did you get any pushback from the task force?"

"Nothing serious. My colleague was freaked when he saw the girls there after hours, especially since this was the first meeting he'd observed between Miss Davis and her superior at city hall," Elise said. "But he was able to get them away without any damage done."

"Speaking of, how did that meeting go?"

"Later," Elise said, glancing around at the nearby patrons.

"Right. Marilee's finding us a private booth, so let's save the rest of this little chat for there."

Soon, the three of them clustered around a booth in the far-right corner of the dining area, burgers, chicken sandwiches, fries, and drinks spread out before them. "So, what more can you tell us about the meeting at city hall last night?" Taylor asked, Marilee sitting expectantly by her side.

Elise took a bite of her burger, glancing around at the nearest patrons, sitting three booths away. "We have a suspect," she almost whispered.

"Really?" Marilee sat back with a start and almost choked on a ketchup-covered fry.

"Who?" Taylor asked.

"The assistant city manager."

"What's *he* being investigated for?" Marilee asked.

"He may be falsifying medical reports for extra payments. The feds have asked us to check out that possibility," Elise replied. "At this point, we haven't ruled out anything or anyone, but something bad's going on. However, we don't see any definite connection between the scams that some residents have reported to you and our fraud case. So I've been instructed to share information with you on the condition that you don't include city hall in your inquiries."

"One government agency defrauding another is just disgusting. Why, there oughta be a law," Marilee said.

"There *is* a law. And we're trying to enforce it," Elise said. "We appreciate you alerting us to the situation at Silverado, Marilee. And we'll stay out of your way if you'll stay out of ours. Of course, we'll be there if you need law enforcement."

"Thanks. Do you need anything besides discretion from us?"

Elise took a bite of her burger, then a long swig of her drink. "As you may have noticed, New Eden's police chief has more than one blind spot."

Taylor and Marilee glanced at each other and nodded solemnly. "Yes," Taylor said. "He's obviously technologically challenged, and that thing he has with women really must make your job more difficult, Elise."

"That's why I signed up to work with the Elder Abuse Task Force. My future on the New Eden Police Force is rather dim." She ate a fry. "I wish I didn't have to tell you this. He's not going to investigate the situation at Silverado. If you want to nail your crook, somebody will have to pay the next bribe. That way, maybe you can catch him with the loot."

"You have my sympathies trying to work for that jerk, but I hate to see more elders lose their money," Marilee said.

"I know. And I hate that it has to be that way. But in this situation, our hands are tied at the local level. If you can catch him with the money, it's possible that it could be returned."

"I see." Taylor took a deep breath. "But I'm with Marilee. I hate to see another of those nice people get robbed in broad daylight. Just because they have some money doesn't mean some crook has the right to steal it. We have to take a chance, or we'll never catch the culprit!"

Elise took a long, last drink of her Dr Pepper. "I agree. We have to stop elder abuse."

Chapter XIII

Another Victim

"Sorry I'm late, Edith. Taylor and I intended to ride together, but at the last minute she had to drop off some paperwork for a case at the courthouse. She should be along soon."

"That's fine, Marilee. Welcome to our weekly special meal, meant to advertise the fine food we dine on."

"I'm glad to be here. Edith, I hope I won't need rehabilitation or long-term care any time soon. At our age, though, you can't be too sure." Marilee knocked on her own head with her knuckles.

Edith surveyed the dining room. "Why don't we order when Taylor gets here? That way, you and I can catch up some more. Besides sleuthing, what's up with you these days, Marilee?"

"I'm beginning to think sleuthing is the easiest part of elderhood, Edith." She squeezed her longtime friend's hand. "How have you been feeling lately?"

Edith raised her fist in a gesture of victory, as if they were still back in Austin cheering on their beloved Longhorns. "The doctors are talking about moving me from medical supervision to long-term care." She lowered her hand and gripped Marilee's. "That would be a step in the right direction, but I want to return to independent living. Soon."

"You scared me. I thought you might say you want to return

to Africa. Whew. I'm relieved that you don't plan to leave us again."

"I might pay Ghana a farewell visit to wind up a few things, but my days of practicing medicine nonstop are over." She waved to a group of women sitting at a nearby table. "In fact, the little bit of sleuthing I've been doing with you two these last few weeks has been invigorating." She took a deep breath. "Do the two of you have a vacancy on your amateur sleuthing team?"

"That sounds fabulous, Edith. I'm sure Taylor would love to talk with you about a permanent position." She glanced up. "And here she comes now."

Taylor hurried into the dining room and pulled out a chair. "Well, I'm finally here."

Marilee covered Taylor's hand with hers. "Slow down, sweetheart. It won't do your digestion or your heart any good to bolt the special meal we're having today." She squeezed Taylor's hand, then let go. "Let's enjoy ourselves for an hour or so."

"Yes," Edith added. "This is a chance to savor another meal together."

"You're right, Edith," Taylor said. "I need to learn to slow down, and this is a perfect time to start. Let's see. I'll have the special salad listed on the menu. How about you two?"

Edith and Marilee nodded their agreement, though Marilee arched a brow as she informed a nearby server. Taylor was obviously itching to get back to work.

"Back your ears," Edith said when their salads arrived, her eyes full of mischief.

After they finished eating, Taylor took a drink of water. "What have you heard in the beauty salon lately, Edith? Any more distraught residents being waylaid for money?"

Edith's expression was indecipherable. "As a matter of fact, I was in there this morning." She turned her head slightly from side to side, then said, "Thanks for noticing my fresh do, my sisters." Marilee gasped and opened her mouth to apologize, but Edith held up her hand.

"While I was finishing up, my new friend Camille opened the door to the beauty shop, made eye contact, and mouthed something I didn't quite get." Edith toyed with her napkin. "But her eyes were red, and she appeared to have been crying." Edith frowned. "I thought I'd go by her room after we finish our meal."

"By all means!" Taylor said, halfway pushing back her dining room chair. "I wish I could join you, but I have an appointment with a client." She looked over at Marilee. "Can you go with Edith to hear what her friend has to say?"

"Sure. I'd like that." She touched Taylor's arm. And, by the way, Edith might be interested in being a Senior Sleuth."

Taylor gave Edith a thumbs-up.

"She doesn't plan to return to Africa. Isn't that great news?"

Edith acted mock-aggrieved. "You people around here talk about Africa as if it were a third-world country. That's wrong in so many ways. First, Africa is a continent, and many of the countries in Africa have risen above the label third world. Besides, victimizing defenseless elders in nursing care sounds emphatically third world to me. Where are the police when we need them?"

"I'm sure they're relieved to have us focus on the hoaxes," Taylor said. "At least our friend Elise Mora is. When we talked with her, she regretted that we might have to pay a bribe to catch the crook." She shook her head. "It's hard to accept, but the Elder Abuse Task Force is rather busy, and the local police aren't interested. Our chief believes he has bigger fish to fry. So Elise asked for our help on this one." Taylor gave a thumbs-up. "And speaking of asking for help, yes, Edith, we'd be thrilled to have you join the team. When you're up to it, of course."

"I'm already up for helping my neighbor Camille," she said. "She was so kind to me before I could get around—visiting, bringing me snacks, watching TV with me in the evenings. Why, here she is. Camille, dear, come join us. I want you to meet my good friends Taylor Bradford and Marilee Connor. This is Camille Hebert."

Taylor stood and shook hands with Camille. "I'm so glad to meet you. You've been a good friend to Edith. And I'm sorry that I have to meet and run. I have an appointment with a client at my office, but I hope we'll have another chance soon to get better acquainted." She turned and hurried out of the dining room.

Marilee, also standing, greeted Camille with a warm, two-handed shake and gestured for her to sit down. "A lot of the other diners have left, so why don't we visit here a few minutes?"

"All right," Camille said. "Although I'd hoped to talk with Miss Taylor about a problem." Her eyes were red and about to overflow.

"Don't worry," Edith said. "Although Taylor is the attorney in our sleuthing group, Marilee is, and always has been, the one who'll take time to listen. And besides, I'm almost assured of a sleuthing position as soon as I'm able to claim it. But, Camille, what in the world has upset you so much?"

"Oh, okay." Camille sat down, grabbing a napkin to dab at her eyes.

Marilee touched her forearm sympathetically. "What's going on, Camille?"

She took a deep breath. "I've heard through the beauty-parlor grapevine that some of us have gotten messages, apparently from young relatives, that they're in trouble or in jail or kidnapped and need lots of money. But when my grandson, my only remaining relative here in Texas, called, I didn't doubt for a minute that he was in trouble. He's always been quite a rascal, though a lovable one." She frowned. "However, I did doubt that he thought I had enough money to resolve the situation. He was always asking me for some, and most of the time I could afford to give him only a fraction of what he requested."

She rested her head on her fist. "But when he told me to ask my cousin Laurence for the money, I knew something was fishy." She frowned. "My grandson has never met, or even heard of, my cousin Laurence, who's truly quite wealthy. I live in Texas because we had a terrible falling-out with the Louisiana family before I was born, and my mother and her not-quite-husband were at the center of the trouble." She raised her eyebrows. "They moved to Texas, married, and broke all ties to the Louisiana kin." Camille blushed.

"Well, that might have been something to be ashamed of when it happened, but today it wouldn't upset much of anybody," Marilee said.

"Thanks for that," Camille said. "But the only Louisiana relative who ever reached out to poor Mother was a much-younger cousin Laurence. She got letters from him occasionally, one of which she showed me and later urged me to burn."

Camille stopped. "But I didn't. Instead, I contacted him, and we developed a friendship." Her voice grew stronger. "We talked by phone and, later, by FaceTime. He's the one who told me about the history of my Louisiana relatives." She paused again.

When Marilee finally realized Camille wanted a sip of water, she pushed her untouched glass toward her. "Do go on, Camille."

"I was the only one in Texas who knew him, and I never told anyone."

"So how in the world did the extortionist know to mention your cousin Laurence's name?" Edith asked.

Camille sipped her water slowly, wrinkling her forehead. "Come to think of it, I identified him on the financial information form that Silverado required before I moved in. My long-term health insurance covered the cost of living here, but the assistant administrator who registered me insisted that I list someone to cover any extra costs. I found the request intrusive, so I provided only the first name of my cousin. Cousin Laurence, Natchitoches Parish, Louisiana. I hoped they'd never be able to find him."

"But maybe they did," Marilee said. "Our assistant administrator *is* a piece of work. I just had an idea. Camille, did the voice on the phone give you any instructions about how much money to gather and where to deliver it?"

Camille raised her head with more focus. "Yes. I nearly left out that part, which is probably the most important. He told me he wanted thousands and thousands of dollars, in cash." She sighed. "But then he said he'd have to call back at six o'clock to tell me exactly how much and where to deliver it. I had started to inform him how totally impossible that would be when he told me again to ask Cousin Laurence for it and hung up."

Marilee stared at Camille and Edith. "This could be exactly the case we need to smash this vicious ring of criminals! I'll call Taylor right away and let her know she needs to get here at once." Marilee began to jump up and then used the tabletop to push herself the rest of the way. "Let's go to your room, Edith, so I can make that call in private and avoid distressing these few late diners. And as we go, I'll fill Camille in with what I've been learning about artificial intelligence speech synthesizers. I think that's what we're up against here."

❖

Half an hour later, Taylor knocked, then walked into Edith's room. "I thought my client was having an emergency with her estranged husband. Little did I know that the real uproar was here all along."

Edith said, "We tried our best to reassure Camille that we'd take care of this situation and that her grandson is completely safe and most likely doesn't know what's going on. In fact, we tried to call him so she could talk to him, but he didn't answer our call. She said he's probably in Las Vegas, gambling, and that sometimes he doesn't respond for days when she tries to contact him." Edith took a deep breath.

"Sounds like she's better off without him," Marilee said. "I suppose it's hard to imagine being almost totally without any family, though that's also the situation I'm in. I'm so glad Taylor's made me part of hers."

"And you're certainly welcome," Taylor said. "I have more than enough cousins to share. So how's Camille feeling now?"

"A bit better," Edith said. "I told her I'd check on her after she rests a while. She's very anxious and distressed about this invasion of her privacy. Obviously, she's never come to terms with her lifelong estrangement from her Louisiana family. Not to mention her very fragile medical condition. I think she needs some doctor's attention, as well as some emotional support. So I'll keep a close eye on her and try to keep things as calm as possible."

"I'm so glad she's in such good hands." Marilee squeezed Edith's arm gently. "What's our next step, Taylor?"

"I do intend to get together whatever I can of the amount of cash they demand and prepare to help apprehend whoever comes to pick up the loot."

Marilee hugged Taylor. "You're my hero, but I don't want you doing anything foolish. This crook could be dangerous."

"I bet this crook doesn't know I have a black belt in karate and that I work out at the gym. I may be small, but I pack a powerful punch."

Marilee widened her eyes. "I didn't know that either. What other surprises do you plan to spring on me?" She gripped Taylor's left upper arm and raised a brow. "Mmm. You're not lying, are you?"

Taylor fake-scowled, and Marilee couldn't keep from smiling. "Edith," she then said. "Why don't you drop in on Camille to see if she's feeling any better and, if not, maybe ask the staff to call the doctor."

Now Taylor was pacing rapidly around the small room, and Marilee went to her, put an arm around her, and asked, "Wouldn't you like to rest for a while?"

Then they sat side by side on Edith's sofa after Edith headed to Camille's room.

"Thanks, sweetie," Taylor said after a few minutes. "My blood pressure is grateful for your concern. What a crazy day this has turned into."

❖

At five fifteen, Camille lay in her small bed, and Edith, her stethoscope carefully hidden in her robe pocket, stood beside her. Marilee had found the only available chair, so when Taylor burst in scowling, Marilee wasn't surprised to hear her say, "Edith, may Marilee and I use your room for a quick strategy session?" Edith frowned, probably because she was disappointed at not being included, but apparently her dedication to Camille kept her from refusing permission. "Of course. Go right ahead," she said. "But, here. Be sure to take Camille's mobile. That's the number they'll be calling."

"Great thought, Sleuth," Taylor said, and Edith brightened at the compliment.

"Did you call Elise?" Marilee asked as soon as they walked out into the hall.

Taylor scowled. "She made it pretty plain that we should take care of this ourselves until the swindler has the cash." She threw her head back. "Isn't that what Nancy Drew would do?"

Marilee couldn't resist giving a small smile. "Of course it is. And just think of all the years of experience we have on her. She was the age of Zooey and Gloria, so our team is double the trouble hers was."

Taylor returned her smile with a larger one. "That's the spirit. We'll make this bad guy regret he ever tangled with us."

Just then, Camille's cell rang, and they ducked into Edith's room for some privacy. Taylor answered with a very brief "hello" while putting the phone on speaker.

A slightly garbled voice said, "Gammy, these guys mean business. They want forty thousand in small bills to be picked up at the front door of your residence at six o'clock tomorrow night. If you call Cousin Laurence now, he should be able to get the cash to you in time."

The phone went dead, and the two of them glared at each other with combined disgust and dismay. Taylor spoke first. "Okay. I'll get with my banker and arrange for the cash."

Marilee turned to Taylor. "We need to make sure we keep

tabs on where the money goes. Could we arrange for someone to discreetly—repeat, discreetly—tail the car?"

"Why don't we see if we can talk Zooey and Gloria into following that guy? Maybe using my Karmann Ghia to tail him would add some incentive. I bet our junior sleuths couldn't resist. After all, they're Nancy Drew's age and would probably love the excitement and intrigue involved."

"Are you sure, Taylor? Even though they're both legally adults, shouldn't we clear this plan with their parents? I don't want to upset them, even though the girls shouldn't be in close contact with whoever makes the pickup. That person might even be a teenager, too."

"Good idea. I'll touch base with Zooey's parents. Then, if we get the go-ahead, we'll get the girls' opinion of the plan. And if they promise to be really careful, it should work. And we need as much visual evidence as we can get about the bag man, his vehicle, and his destination."

"That's where I come in," Marilee said. "I'll use one of my husband's digital cameras and position myself where I can get a clean shot of whoever comes to pick up the money. And I'll also just snap away at whatever I can see that might prove useful."

"Excellent. You're a great partner," Taylor said.

"I better go tell Camille and Edith generally what's going on. And I'll make a real effort to try to get Edith to make sure neither of them talks about this with *anyone*. Though I don't know how successful I'll be."

"Good luck with that. Let's walk down to Camille's room together. Maybe we can head off more gossip."

CHAPTER XIV

Trapping the Villains

Taylor ended her phone conversation and turned to Marilee, who was just putting a batch of cornbread into the oven for their late supper.

"How'd it go?" Marilee asked.

"My banker is a stand-up guy. He promised to have the cash in used twenty-dollar bills ready for me to pick up at four o'clock tomorrow afternoon. I just need to have a bag big enough to hold all that cash."

"Okay. It's my turn. I'll touch base with the girls." Picking up her phone, Marilee texted Zooey.

Would you and Gloria be interested in tailing a crook tomorrow about six?

YES.

Great. Meet us at Bradford's Arbor at 4:15. Taylor said you could drive the Ghia. And be sure your cell is fully charged.

WE WOULDN'T MISS THIS FOR THE WORLD!!!!!

In a bit, the oven buzzer began to sound. "If you'll slice the tomatoes, I'll get the cornbread and set the table."

Taylor paused on her way to the basket of tomatoes Lois had shared from a local farmers' market haul. "I hope we still have what it takes to pull off our first Senior Sleuth case. Or should we just retire to our rocking chairs on the front porch instead?"

Marilee gazed at Taylor fondly, faintly surprised. Taylor usually thought she could succeed in anything she set her mind to. Or at least that's how she'd always appeared to Marilee. As they prepared their meal together, Marilee said, "A friend in Austin sent me an article from the *New England Journal of Medicine* that indicated lots of good stuff about the brains of older people. For example, the brain of a healthy person sixty or more is in some ways better than that of a younger person, including that the two hemispheres of an older brain may have less difficulty communicating with each other." She pushed up her glasses to show that she was serious. "The article also said that we're more likely to make good decisions with age. Maybe we have a good shot at making this Senior Sleuths venture work."

"Dearest science person, I hate to have to say this. When I heard about that article, I tried to authenticate it. Sadly, the *NEJM* never published anything like it. But let's agree that it *should* be true. How about a friendly kiss on each cheek to show that all our hemispheres are eager to collaborate?"

"Definitely." They settled into their supper.

In fifteen minutes, putting the dishes into the dishwasher, Marilee stopped and stared at the two knives and forks she was holding. "Let's reconsider my positioning myself behind the bushes at the front of the property to take pictures of the driver and his car." She bent down and jabbed the utensils into a nearly full cutlery holder.

Taylor wiped their cast-iron skillet.

"What if the sprinkler system comes on? I'll be borrowing an expensive telephoto lens." Marilee grabbed a sponge and rubbed the black enamel top of their old gas kitchen stove.

Taylor didn't respond.

"And for another thing, what about my knees?" Marilee whirled around, then pointed down at her legs. "Have you considered that I'm walking around with two prosthetic knees? If I had to kneel to hide, I might never get up again. Did you consider that?"

Taylor finished wiping off the kitchen counters, then washed and dried her hands. "Relax, sweetheart." She guided her over to a nearby stool. "For starters, I don't remember discussing where you would position yourself."

Marilee stared at her as if she'd lost her mind. "But—"

"And I never said that bushes were a good hiding place for anyone, much less my shiny-new-kneed partner." She chuckled at her own joke. "You're letting your imagination run away with you, dear one."

Marilee didn't move for a while, and then she took several deep breaths. "I agree with you."

"So where could you get good pics? The top of the building?" Taylor smirked.

After another few breaths, Marilee slowly stood from the stool she'd been perched on, trying to calm her rampaging mind. "Obviously I've been worrying about it, or I wouldn't have gotten so ramped up," she said. "This is important, and I want to do it right. Being a Senior Sleuth obviously entails more thought and practice than I expected. I'm just not used to all this pressure yet."

She picked up a dish towel and slowly redried the pan Taylor had dried earlier. "How about I sit in my Rogue in the Silverado parking lot with a bag from Whataburger, pretending to be on a dinner break? I could keep the camera out of sight until the driver is focused on you at the front door and won't notice me. I'll need a bean bag or a small pillow to support and steady the lens. That might work better."

"Okay. You win." Taylor kissed her cheek. "Even though I'm sure I never said it, I take back my mistaken suggestion that you hide in the shrubbery. And I'll never overestimate your knees again." She held out her hand. "How about a little TV? It's been a long day, and I'd love to see the latest episode of *Vera*. Maybe we can get a few pointers from her."

❖

"I'm heading to Walmart first thing this morning," Taylor called. "Do you need anything while I'm there?" She tapped on the bathroom door to make sure Marilee had heard her.

Suddenly, it opened, and there stood Marilee. Her short hair lay in damp, loose curls, the ones on the back of her neck like a row of commas. "No. You go ahead. But what do you plan to buy there? You never just go to shop around, like I do."

"When I called my banker last night, I asked him what type of bag would be best to hold forty thousand dollars in used twenties."

"Good move. And what did he suggest?"

"A twenty-by-twenty-inch soft-sided one, as inconspicuous as possible. So I guess I'll check in the luggage section, or maybe where they sell computer accessories. Do those sound like good places to at least start?"

"I'm proud of you, Taylor. That's exactly where I'd try. Good move for a non-shopper like you."

"Thanks. I'm trying to learn to be more home centered. Do you need anything while I'm in Walmart?"

"No. But thanks for asking. I like this new version of you." Marilee ran her fingers through her still-wet curls. "I located my husband's lightweight digital camera last night and took several shots in various settings around my room to make sure I still know how to use it. To my knowledge, I've never mentioned that I was his assistant for years. Obviously, if I'm not very near the action, I'll need to use a telephoto lens."

Taylor gave her a thumbs-up. "Good thought. I vaguely remember you saying something last night about needing to borrow an expensive one. Is that correct?"

"It is. My husband never bought one. But I just called a photographer friend of his who lives out at Sunset Lake, and he said I can borrow his for a few days."

"Great. You're really on the ball, Marilee. Do we need to drive to his place and pick it up?"

"No. Luckily, he has a dental appointment here in town this

afternoon, so he said he'd drop it off about one. You go on to Walmart, and I'll check on Edith and the girls. Have you talked to their parents yet?"

"May I remind you that Nancy Drew and her cohorts were the same age as Zooey and Gloria, who are old enough to serve in the US Army or any other branch of service," Taylor said.

"I'll have a serious talk with them before tonight's caper and find out if they want us to mention this to their parents. I'll also emphasize how careful they need to be when they drive the Ghia."

"Sure thing. See you soon."

Marilee returned to putting on her light makeup, then located Edith's information in her phone and connected with her. "How's it going out at Silverado?" she asked.

"Oh. I'm so glad you touched base. I'm distracting myself by watching over Camille."

"How's she doing today?"

Marilee studied herself in the mirror. She wanted to appear as authoritative as possible if she somehow encountered this low-life criminal who preyed on the older generation.

"Camille still seems weak, but all the support she's been receiving has heartened her."

Marilee shook herself out of her reverie. "That's great news, Edith. You two get some rest, and don't worry about us. The Senior Sleuths are in high gear."

Edith smiled. "I'm glad to hear it and am sending you support and gratitude for everything you're trying to do."

❖

At four o'clock, Taylor picked up the money, saw that it fit nicely in the new bag, and arrived home to find Marilee, Zooey, Gloria, and Lois in the driveway, waiting for her.

"Tay, I thought you'd never get here! Where have you been?"

"At the bank picking up my hard-earned money and making

sure it fits in this." She held up a black, nondescript computer bag labeled *Microsoft*. "How's this?"

"Perfect. No one would ever guess it's full of thousands of dollars in cash," Zooey said. "Can I peek inside? I've never seen that much money before."

"For just a minute."

Marilee laughed at how wide Zooey's eyes grew.

"You, too, Gloria. That way you'll both know why you need to be really careful. This isn't what they call 'chump change.' It's serious money, and we want to make sure we get it back."

"Yes, ma'am," they said.

"Thanks for trusting us enough to let us be part of this operation," Zooey said. "And I can't wait to drive your Ghia. But I've been thinking about it and really need to take a spin around the block to make sure I know how to drive your old foreign car." Zooey was practically jumping with excitement.

"Well, then, why don't you two hop in. I'll get in the back, though I won't be able to stay in it very long because it's so darn small. Gloria, you take the passenger seat and understudy Zooey in case you have to take over." Taylor walked around her prized blue convertible, its sleek lines never failing to delight her. "And it's *vintage,* not old, mind you. And brilliantly maintained, which is a necessity for this baby."

As the others watched, Zooey—significantly larger than Taylor—slid into the driver's side. She immediately pushed back the very reluctant seat and coaxed the seat belt to let out more length than ever before. It took a few minutes, and Taylor started to get out of the narrow plywood platform that constituted the Ghia's snug "back seat."

Just then, though, Zooey turned the key, and the car roared to life. But as she was searching for drive, the shifter dropped into reverse, and Zooey's foot fell off the clutch. The car jolted back, and *wham*. It hit something and died. Both girls turned around, pale, apparently to see whether Taylor had survived. Always petite, Taylor's crumpled body must have looked vanishingly small, but she groaned. Thankfully, she was alive and unharmed. "What the hell?" she grumbled.

Zooey turned bright pink as apologies tumbled from her mouth. "I'm so sorry, Miss Taylor. I thought I knew how to drive a stick shift. I don't know what happened."

Gloria was staring out the rearview mirror on her side. "I hope we didn't smash Miss Marilee's Rogue." She opened her door to help Taylor crawl out, and Zooey met them at the back of the car.

"Thank heavens!" Taylor said. "The curb stopped you before you could take out the Rogue. Nice work, Zooey. Should we give Gloria a shot at driving?"

"Oh, no, please, Miss Taylor," Gloria said. "I've never driven a car like this. Please give Zooey a second chance. She's really a good driver normally. She's just not used to a stick shift."

"What's your opinion, Zooey? I'm game if you are," Taylor said, stretching her legs to make sure they still functioned. "I had a few false starts the first time I drove a car like this, too."

The pink in Zooey's cheeks began to recede. "Yes, please. I'd like to try again. I remember now about the clutch and where reverse is. I should do better this time. But maybe you could just watch me through the window while I get started, so you don't have to curl up in that tiny space back there again."

"That's a good idea. It's so cramped, I couldn't see much anyway. Okay, you two. Mount up and give her another go," Taylor said gamely.

This time the car moved quickly around the driveway and onto the side street next to Bradford's Arbor. The Ghia was soon out of sight, but the smooth sounds of shifting reassured Taylor that this shake-down cruise was a success. She turned to Lois. "Will you be at home this evening? I'd appreciate your being on call in case something goes wrong with this plan."

"Sure. I'll be studying, but I'll have my phone on and be ready to respond if needed. What could go wrong?" she said and took a deep breath.

"Nothing, I hope. I just wanted to be sure you'd be available as backup tonight."

"We both have come to rely on your availability and your ability to respond to new situations," Marilee said. "Thank you, Lois, for your help."

"I'm delighted to serve as your backup. Just give me a call," Lois said. "By the way, Marilee, if you're planning to take pictures from the Rogue, the windows could use a quick clean-up. I'll be happy to do that, if you'll let me."

"I'll be forever in your debt, Lois. Car washing isn't easy on the arthritis. Thanks so much!" Marilee gave her a quick hug and headed back into the house.

❖

"Are you sure those girls are well hidden?" Marilee asked as Taylor entered Camille's room at Silverado. "I'm glad you let them use your car. They had Zooey's van at the city hall, and we can't be sure it wasn't noticed."

"I checked on the way in," Taylor said. "The girls are behind a clump of trees near the road leading to Silverado, and whichever way the car turns, they'll be able to follow it. They've promised that Gloria will have her cell on the whole time and that they'll keep us informed about their every move."

"Great. Now all we have to do is wait thirty-five minutes," Marilee said.

Edith spoke up. "As an associate member of the Senior Sleuths, I've managed to round up two additional chairs, so why don't we all sit down while we wait. Camille, let me help you sit up a little higher. Would you like to sip on some water?"

Camille nodded, and Edith handed her a Styrofoam cup with a straw.

Taylor said, "That makes me thirsty, although I'm not the least bit hungry. Why don't I pop down to the dining room for a glass of lemonade for all of us?"

"Make mine unsweet iced tea, please," Marilee said.

"I'd take a cup of hot chamomile tea, if you don't mind," Edith said.

Taylor tensed her jaw slightly as the orders for drinks poured in. As she turned to leave the room, Marilee whispered in her ear, "Thanks for making time to ask what others need, dear one. Full points for today!"

Taylor's jaw muscles relaxed, and she smacked a quick kiss on Marilee's cheek.

CHAPTER XV

Chasing Villains

"It's five forty-five, time for me and my money bag to get to the front door and for Marilee to go sit in the Rogue," Taylor told Marilee, Edith, and Camille as they waited in the Silverado lobby for the action to begin.

Wearing a dark suit and white shirt, Taylor felt in control of the coming transaction. She planned to confront this thief and try to reason with him. Was he an amateur, inexperienced and working alone, or was he part of a large organization that would stop at nothing? How could she best convince him to change his mind and abandon this scheme to steal from innocent old people?

"Roger." Marilee wrapped her arms around Taylor and hugged her as if she might never see her again. Sweat trickled down Taylor's side. To be honest, she'd much rather be sitting with Marilee enjoying the cool of the evening breeze than getting ready to confront a thief.

"Best of luck," Edith and Camille chorused as they went to their rooms. "Keep us posted."

Once they all were in position, the minutes dragged by endlessly. Taylor tried to stand still, but she couldn't keep from pacing in circles in the large area near the front entryway. What if the guy showed up, and something spooked him? Would he shoot her? Surely he wouldn't be carrying in broad daylight. But, after all, this was Texas. She wasn't ready to die. She'd just been given a second chance with the woman she cared for more than she'd known. And they were just getting started on the adventures she hoped would last as long as they lived.

At six o'clock sharp, Gloria's number rang into Taylor's cell. Taylor grabbed it like it was a call from the President of the United States.

"I believe I see the car approaching." Gloria sounded much calmer than Taylor would have been as a teenager involved in a chancy situation like this.

"The car isn't much." Gloria spoke softly. "A red Ford pickup, but we didn't get the license number. I'll be sure to do that when he leaves. The driver is a man, by the way. Anglo, dark-haired, clean-cut. Not a criminal type at all. More like an accountant or a pharmacist. Very professional. Over."

Taylor gazed through the glass-paneled front door and spotted the pickup pulling up in front of Silverado. "He's almost at the entrance now, Gloria. You girls be careful. I'll keep this line open, and you can tell me what he does from a safe distance. Do you understand?"

What if something happens to one of them? They're my responsibility. Have I taken every possible precaution to make sure they won't be harmed?

The red pickup stopped under the large, covered entrance, the motor still running, and Taylor hoisted the bag full of money she'd placed on the small round table near the front door. How could something so light be so valuable? And what if things went south and somehow she lost this money? It wasn't just pocket change. She'd had to cash in a recently matured CD to raise this much on such short notice.

As the driver remained behind the wheel, Taylor opened one of the double doors and stepped out. "Stop right there." She used her official courtroom voice. "I have your cash here, but as an officer of the court, I demand that you cease this illegal activity right now. Drive away immediately, and we'll all forget this ever happened. Do not compound your extortion attempt by accepting this money and becoming a common thief. The court doesn't take such activities lightly."

Taylor focused. The driver was wearing a ski mask!

"Officer of the court, my foot!" the masked driver said.

Taylor detected a slight tremor in his voice.

"Put the bag down and back away," he said. "As even you must be able to see, I'm much bigger than you are and can easily take that bag from you."

Taylor studied the driver. She had a hard time making out much about him, since he was masked and still in the car. Taking a chance was foolish. She wanted to live, not let a greedy thief knock her down.

"Okay," she said. "I'll leave the bag here near the front door and step back inside. Just pick it up and drive away. But I still strongly advise you to turn around and go home."

"No way." The man snarled the words. "I'm not getting out of this car while you're nearby. Come put the bag in front of the driver's side wheel. Then go back inside and pretend all this never happened. Do not call the police."

Taylor was tempted to rush out to the vehicle and try to force him out of it, but, even with her karate skills, he was so much bigger and stronger than she was, he could probably push her away—if he didn't actually punch her—and drive off. Besides, they really needed the police to catch him with the money. Why cause any further delay? Her heart pounding and sweat dripping in her eyes, she moved toward the front of the truck.

At the same time, the man opened his door and stood beside it. Taylor dropped the black bag as instructed. The man stood there while she returned to the front door and entered the facility. Taylor turned to watch him snatch the bag, climb back into the pickup, put it in gear, and leave.

"Did you hear that, Gloria?" she said into the phone. "He's on his way out. Get the license plate if you can! I'll head for Marilee's car as soon as possible. Be careful!"

Taylor watched through the front door, and as soon as the pickup disappeared from her sight, she called Edith. "The guy took the money, the girls will follow him, and Marilee and I will be right behind the girls." Then she rushed out the door to the side parking lot, where Marilee sat waiting for her in the Rogue, its engine running.

Taylor huffed as she tumbled into the passenger's seat. "Did you think of driving to pick me up?"

"Did you think of asking to be picked up?" a not-at-all-rebuked Marilee asked. They both grinned, and Marilee headed out of the parking area. "Ask Gloria which way to turn when we get to the intersection, please," Marilee said as she thoughtfully accelerated above her usual careful pace. "I can't see them from here."

"Gloria, got that? We need some directions," Taylor said.

Gloria responded quickly. "It's really easy. Just drive as if you were heading for the new high school. We'll let you know if his route changes."

"That piece of information might help you locals," Marilee said, sounding tense. "But I don't know where the new high school is. Help! Now!"

"Be calm." Taylor patted Marilee's tightly clenched arm. "Just stick with me. I'll get us there."

Marilee sped up, then slowed, watching the road ahead of her carefully.

"I'm really glad you feel up to driving. All of this has shaken me up a little."

"I'm having a ball. Haven't had this much excitement in years. Of course, a steady diet of it might get old fast."

For the next half hour, conversation came to a halt. Occasionally, Taylor reported a turn that Gloria had taken. But other than that, the streets of New Eden soon gave way to pot-holed country roads and looming huge pines and oak trees. Although Marilee wasn't familiar with the route, she began to complain that they were driving in circles. Taylor confirmed this possibility with the girls, who added that they thought the general direction was toward Kilgore. Before long, even Marilee said that she recognized the outskirts of the small town. They were definitely in Kilgore, fifteen miles from New Eden.

When Zooey and Gloria slowed down, Marilee stepped on her brakes.

CHAPTER XVI

Giggles

"Guess what? He's slowing down. Looks like he's pulling into a driveway. Can you believe he lives in Kilgore, Texas?" Gloria sounded excited, weary, and bewildered.

"Be very careful, girls," Taylor said. "Just keep on driving until you're sure he can't see you. We're a block or so behind you. Let me know if you can read the street address. When you're out of sight, find a place to park. Marilee will pull up behind you soon. Don't get out yet."

"We saw his truck in the driveway but couldn't make out the street number. Sorry," Gloria replied. "It might be written on the curb. We didn't have time to check there."

"Yes," Taylor said. "I see the truck. We're just passing it now, and you're right. The number is 2515. Stay put, but it's okay to celebrate. You girls did a great job."

Taylor turned to Marilee. "You should see them soon. Try to park next to them. But before we tell them to get out of the Ghia, why don't you take time to look through the pictures you took back at Silverado."

"Aw, shoot!" Marilee exclaimed. "My pictures are just fine, but the guy's wearing a mask. We still have no idea who we followed."

"Yes. I noticed the mask, too, but in all the excitement, I forgot to mention it."

"Maybe Elise would help us identify him if we sent her the license plate number and address," Marilee said.

"Well, I'm not sure. She was pretty clear about keeping our cases separate. But we do have a bad guy with the money. Maybe she'd want to know how we're doing."

As Marilee began texting Elise, Taylor returned her attention to the girls. "We're parked right behind you, but please stay where you are a few more minutes. As soon as Marilee sends the info we have to Elise, we'll ask you to come get in the backseat of her SUV one at a time. We need to be inconspicuous. Got that, Glo?"

"Yes, Miss Tay," Gloria said, her voice shaky. "Whatever you say. But you better make it quick. We're so excited we're about to explode."

Her tongue sticking out of the side of her mouth as she concentrated on forwarding the necessary information, Marilee hit send. "There we go. I've sent the street address and his license plate number. That should give Elise something to work with. Can we let the girls join us now, Taylor?"

"Absolutely. Gloria, did you hear that? How about you come first and get in behind me, and when you're in with the door closed, Zooey can make her way over."

After the girls completed the maneuver, Taylor and Marilee turned to the bouncing backseat, full of two extremely jubilant junior sleuths.

"How did we do?" Zooey asked. "It was great to drive a car with some pickup. My big old van could never have kept up the pace when the bad guy sped out of town, and he certainly would have spotted it on the country roads he used to make sure he wasn't being followed. But we fooled him! We know these roads well, so we didn't have to keep him in sight all the time. It didn't look like he ever saw anyone behind him. Right, Glo?"

"Right!" Gloria was beaming with pleasure.

"I totally agree. You two have the makings of top-notch

sleuths, and you're not even close to eighty years old," Taylor said, chuckling. "Hold on. Here's Elise. Okay if I put you on speakerphone, Elise? All four of us are sitting in the SUV and are dying to know what you can tell us about our bag man."

The car filled with the sound of Elise's guffaws, causing the four of them to stare at each other and shake their heads. Taylor thought their work had been laudable rather than laughable. Frowning, she tried to interrupt Elise's outburst.

"What's so funny? We've just chased a criminal holding a huge bag of money—my money, I might mention—from town through the countryside to another town, without being noticed. You find that hilarious?"

Elise tried to speak but broke out in another round of giggles.

"Get a grip. Please," Taylor said, frowning. "We want to join you if it's that good."

Elise tried again. "You'll never guess who you've caught!" But another explosion of guffaws stopped Elise from explaining what she meant.

Taylor's irritation rose. *What the heck?*

Marilee grabbed Taylor's phone. "Really, Elise. This is torture. Take a deep breath. Count to ten. Envision your worst case. Whatever it takes, you've got a car full of folks who want to know what's going on."

Finally, Elise stifled her sobs long enough to say, "You've caught an undercover policeman. Congratulations. I'm on my way there now, but it'll take a few minutes. Why don't you go get something to eat? I'll meet you in Kilgore as soon as I can get there."

Marilee appeared bewildered as she stared at Taylor and the girls. "What did Elise mean when she said we caught an undercover policeman?"

"Even if he was a policeman, wasn't he acting illegally by receiving ransom money?" Gloria asked.

They obviously all had a lot of questions, but with no one to answer them, they just stared at each other.

Finally, Marilee asked, "Where do y'all want to eat?"

The girls gazed at each other. "Let's go to the Back Porch," Zooey said. "It's not far, and the food's great."

"Sounds good to me," Taylor said. "Girls, do you want to drive my Ghia and let us follow you in the SUV? Unless you've had enough of the convertible for now." She was sure of their answer.

"Oh, please, no, Tay," Zooey begged. "I'm just getting the hang of the stick shift." She paused. "And it would be really good for our reputations for Gloria and me to be seen driving a convertible in Kilgore."

Taylor remembered how she'd felt about cars and popularity sixty years ago, when she was nearer their age. "I guess that'll be fine. Zooey, you and Gloria lead the way. But not too fast. Marilee knows Kilgore better than New Eden, but she may not be clear about how to get to the restaurant from here."

Soon the four of them were sitting in the Back Porch, the sounds of country music filling the air, the smell of hamburgers and chicken fried steak permeating the large dining room. Taylor had seen to it that they were seated in a relatively quiet, secluded corner, but once again using her best officer-of-the-court tone, she reminded everyone in their booth to keep their voices down. As they were settling in, a waitress took their orders for two Cokes, an unsweetened iced tea, and one water.

Taylor said to the group, "I'll bet Dr. Edith would welcome a report. It's taken a lot longer than I thought it would to get off the road. Give me a minute to catch her up." She punched in Dr. Edith's number.

A worried-sounding Edith answered quickly. "Hello. Is that you, Taylor? Whatever has taken so long for you to call? It's after eight o'clock. Everybody here is ready to go to bed, including me."

"We're safe and sound, friend. Please relax. Our money man led the girls and us on a long, tedious back-roads journey to Kilgore. The girls did a great job of following him, and Marilee and I stayed on the phone with them to keep us on their trail. After he parked and went into a house in an ordinary neighborhood, we called Elise." Taylor glanced over at Marilee and gave her a thumbs-up. "We were feeling really proud of our work, but all we could get out of her was giggles. She's on her way here now. We'll make sure she explains what's going on as soon as she gets here." Taylor made sure the rest of the table was following the conversation.

"Tell Edith hi from all of us," Marilee said. The girls waved in the direction of Taylor's phone.

"How's Camille doing? Has the staff doctor seen her this evening?" Taylor asked.

"All is well here. Camille was resting after dinner, so I left her to wait for your call in my room. A staff nurse here has given her something for anxiety, and hopefully that has helped."

"Put up your feet, friend, and we'll update you as soon as we learn something new." Taylor clicked off her phone and put the device face down on the table. Then she turned to the girls, giving them her full attention as they sipped their Cokes.

"Okay. Let's hear how it went, girls. How did you find your first pursuit? Besides successful, that is."

Marilee spoke up. "Yes, very successful, I should say." She saluted them with her glass of tea. "Let's hear it from your perspective."

Zooey winked at Gloria and began. "At first, it was just hot and boring, waiting for him to come and for Taylor to hand over the loot. And by the way, how come you never mentioned the lack of air conditioning in Karmann Ghias? But as soon as we spotted him driving up to Silverado's front door, things got interesting."

"Yeah," Gloria said. "Especially when Miss Taylor told the guy to just give up and go home."

"We could hear their conversation through your cell phone,

Tay, and I was afraid we might hear gunshots next," Zooey added. "But then you let us know he was leaving the nursing home, and we got the car in gear—drive instead of reverse this time—and took off after him."

Gloria giggled, and Zooey made a face at her and continued. "At first, I thought he would just drive around New Eden, but then he got out on the farm-to-market roads, and I made double sure to stay as far back as I could. The only time I got a little closer was when I knew an intersection was coming up." She took a sip of her Coke, beaming proudly.

Gloria wiggled in her seat, like she couldn't stay still or quiet any longer. "It was real exciting," she said, "and you would have been so proud of Zooey's driving." She gazed at Zooey with obvious affection. "Of course, the Ghia is pretty quiet, but it was so hot outside, even at that time of day, we were sure he had his AC on and the windows rolled up." Her grin widened. "We never saw any sign that he even suspected we were following him."

"What did you think when he kept driving through the back roads of Lee County?" Marilee asked.

"Well, I was relieved, at least for a while," Zooey said, frowning slightly. "I knew the gas tank was full when we started today, but I was beginning to get worried when the gauge hit the halfway point, and we were still out in the boonies. Old cars aren't known for their great gas mileage." Zooey held up her hand. "My bad. I mean vintage cars. Right, Tay?"

"Yes, vintage, and no, not known for great gas economy even without air conditioning. By the way, I was relieved, too, when you told us he'd turned into a driveway. But frankly, I was surprised to see that he has such a conventional home in a very ordinary, middle-class neighborhood."

"Me, too," Marilee said. "I expected our bad guy to live in a shack or an abandoned oil-well pumping station, or something else grim."

"He's obviously living pretty well," Gloria added. "Maybe

he's been ripping off old people long enough to become a homeowner."

"What did you make of the fact that he was wearing a mask? Could it mean we might recognize him?" Taylor asked.

"Mask?" Both girls shrieked at once. "He wasn't wearing one when he passed us. We gave you a description, but I certainly didn't recognize him. Did you, Gloria?"

"No, I didn't. But I was sorta tense."

Just then the waitress stopped by to ask if they were ready to order. As usual, Taylor spoke for the group. "Not just yet. We're waiting for a friend. How about another round of drinks, though? And maybe some chips and salsa, just to keep body and soul together until she gets here?"

As the waitress nodded and turned to fill the new order, Taylor's phone rang. When she answered, she motioned the group to be quiet. "Yes, Elise. We're at the Back Porch restaurant, not far from the college. Do you know how to get here? Great! We'll see you in a few minutes. What can we order you to drink?" After Taylor hung up, she said, "Well, at least this time she wasn't laughing so hard she couldn't talk. In fact, she may have sounded a little grim. Anyway, she'll be here soon and can explain everything in person."

When the waitress returned with the chips, salsa, two more Cokes, and pitchers of tea and water, Taylor asked her to bring another glass—of Dr Pepper, this time, and menus for everyone. Finally, they were about to find out what was going on with Elise.

CHAPTER XVII

Giggles Explained

A few minutes later, a somber Elise Mora pulled up a chair to the end of the large booth that the sleuths occupied. Gloria put her Dr Pepper in front of her, and the four of them silently waited for Elise to catch her breath and relay the latest developments.

"Well, the good news is, you weren't in any danger," Elise said.

Taylor stared at her. *What in the world is she talking about?*

Elise still appeared serious. "But I've had to promise never again to let civilians follow an undercover colleague when he's on the job."

Marilee frowned.

"The guy who picked up the money from Taylor this afternoon, the one you two tailed to his home in Kilgore…" She took a big swallow of her drink, and Taylor held her breath, afraid Elise would collapse in giggles again. "He works undercover for the same task force on elder abuse that I do."

Marilee stopped crunching on the chip she'd just taken a bite of, and Zooey and Gloria quit smiling.

"What's more, he'd already seen Zooey and Gloria when they followed Miss Davis to the city hall. Sorry, girls, but he recognized you as soon as he drove into Silverado. Knowing he had to deliver the money to the real bad guy, he slipped on a ski mask and led you around the countryside to his own home."

"You mean he knew all along?" Zooey asked.

"'Fraid so," Elise replied. "He's been undercover, working his way into the confidence of the New Eden assistant city manager, who's been defrauding the government by manipulating the insurance data he gets from Silverado."

"But that's *your* case," Taylor said. "Our case relates to the extortion of Silverado residents. And you said to keep them separate."

"That's the other news of the day. Our two cases aren't separate. We now believe the assistant city manager has two different scams going. So the task force is now involved in both."

"Does it help that Gloria and I know someone from high school who works at Silverado?" Zooey asked. "At first we thought he might be in cahoots with Miss Davis, and we told Taylor and Marilee about him, but since we've gotten to know him better, I think he could help you with your side of the case. He's a computer geek who really wants to help Silverado procedures become more efficient. His name is John, and he works in the basement."

"If you'll text me his number, I'll reach out to him. Thanks." Elise gazed solemnly at the two girls.

Zooey and Gloria sat up straighter.

"The task force I'm part of was created to try to stop elder abuse. Although we initially emphasized the fraud in nursing home management, your investigation uncovered fraud involving individual elders. So the task force has just expanded its mission to include individuals as well as institutions. I think it's important to focus on both aspects. The task force wants to have more impact on the local crimes against our older citizens."

Marilee leaned forward. "And that's also why we've established Senior Sleuths. We'll have even more impact if we can work together."

"As you know," Elise said, "prosecution is always much

easier if we're able to catch a suspect in a criminal act. So that's why our agent led you to his house instead of to the real criminal. We're certain now that the assistant city manager is calling the shots in this case as well, and our guy plans to meet him at Silverado in the morning. Apparently, Miss Davis is demanding a cut. Of course, you absolutely have to keep these plans confidential. Deal?" Elise asked with an earnest expression.

Elise eyed Marilee, Taylor, Zooey, and Gloria in turn. Each of them looked at her seriously.

"We promise," Marilee replied for them all.

The waitress appeared and took their orders, and they busied themselves with their drinks, chips, and salsa. But after she left, Zooey turned to Elise. "Does chasing a criminal make you hungry? I'm starving!"

Marilee spoke up. "Miss Davis wants some of the money from this hoax? What do you know about her role in all this, Elise?"

Elise leaned back in her chair and sipped her Dr Pepper. "So far, the task force suspects she's claiming medical treatments that were never performed. But she may also be complicit in asking elders for money to help relatives. Didn't you say that it's only the wealthier residents who've been hit with these scams?"

Both Gloria and Zooey kept their eyes on Elise. Gloria spoke first. "We're pretty sure they've targeted those who could make the payment. And we think there was a privacy violation in Miss Camille's case."

Taylor explained. "In Camille's case, the caller mentioned a wealthy relative who had been listed as a financial guarantor. Somebody had to have accessed her files to know that. It had to have been Miss Davis or someone in the administration at Silverado. Sounds to me like a violation of privacy, at the very least."

"We're still checking into how and why she's involved," Elise said.

"Pure meanness, if you ask me," Marilee blurted out. "Why

in the world would they employ her to work with elders? She's a walking gloom bomb. Although I do have to admit that she does love her little dog."

Gloria grabbed one of the last chips from the second red plastic basket the waitress had brought them. "Maybe it's more than that. While I've been working around her, I've noticed that not only does she love her dog, but she covers for her assistant, who's not really able to do her work. That's why I was assigned to her office, to take the load off that poor woman. So Miss Davis does have some good points, I suppose." She sipped the last of her second Coke. "But she also seems to have a grudge against anyone who appears to be financially better off than she is. That might have something to do with her childhood..."

Taylor spoke up. "Gloria, that's the longest speech I've ever heard you make. And it makes sense. Good thinking!" She turned to Elise. "The task force should probably investigate any history between Miss Davis and the assistant city manager." Taylor studied her watch. "Let me call Edith back before our food gets here. It's not that late, and I know she's anxious to hear something. I didn't have much to tell her when I called earlier."

Taylor put in the number and soon had Edith on the phone. "If you're still awake enough, we have some news for you, but it's highly confidential."

"Of course," Edith replied. "I'm used to confidentiality. Taylor, what's happening with the money? Did you arrest the thief and get it all back?"

Just then, Taylor's stomach growled, but she registered what Edith had asked her. "Sorry. This has been a really long day, Edith. And now we have to keep everything that's happened under wraps."

"But why?" Edith asked in a businesslike tone.

Taylor took a deep breath. After all, Edith knew everything so far, so it wouldn't be fair not to tell her the rest of what was going on. "It's so hush-hush because the really bad guy hasn't taken possession of the money yet. The guy we followed earlier turned out to be an undercover cop!"

Edith took a deep, noisy breath. "What?"

"I know, and I'll fill you in with all the details later. But until the real bad guy has the money in hand, he isn't clearly implicated in this hoax." Taylor was ready for this night to end. "So, we have to wait until the handover tomorrow."

"When will this nightmare end?" Edith asked. "I think I'll have to let Camille know, because she's been so anxious, but I'll swear her to secrecy. When will I see you two again?"

Her stomach growling, Taylor gazed longingly at the busy waitress. "We'll be at Silverado first thing in the morning. How does that sound?"

"That should be fine. But please don't keep us hanging much longer. This kind of stress isn't good for any of us! Good night to you all. See you bright and early tomorrow."

Just then, the food finally arrived. And after the hubbub of getting the right platter to the right person, a welcome quiet fell over the table. The sounds of the country music again blanketed their booth as all five of them tucked into their meals with quiet intensity. Sleuthing *is* hungry work, Taylor thought.

❖

After her conversation with Taylor, Edith got up from her recliner, adjusted her sleep bonnet, and snapped her white knit robe all the way down. Then she carefully made her way to the door of her room and grasped the handles of her bright-red rollator, the newest gadget she'd been issued to help her walk more easily. This shiny device with wheels and a sitting platform was designed to help her take longer, faster strides and to rest when she reached her destination. The doctors were obviously rewarding her for faithfully following the rehab routines they'd prescribed. This new device encouraged and enabled her to practice more fluid movements.

Soon she was at Camille's door, but the lively conversation she heard coming from the room surprised her. She'd expected Camille to be in bed, ready to go to sleep. After she knocked, the room grew quiet, and Camille called out, "Come on in," which she did. The three other victims at Silverado—Mrs. Richards, Mr. Yandle, and Mrs. Gray—sat crowded together in Camille's small room and gazed up at her eagerly.

Glad that her new rollator came with its own chair, she squeezed into the room. "Hi, everybody. How's your day been?" she asked.

Camille spoke up. "We'll all be a lot better if you can tell us where the money's been going. Have they caught the criminal yet?"

"No. But they're making progress." She cautiously repeated a little of what she'd heard from Taylor, then added, "But you have to promise not to tell a soul until the mastermind is behind bars. Not even your roommate, if you have one. Agreed?"

"Yes. Of course we agree," Camille said. "Please tell us everything you know in detail."

Edith locked her rollator and sat down on its cushioned vinyl seat. "The guy who came here earlier to pick up the money wasn't the brains behind these crimes after all, just a middleman—and an undercover policeman at that." She shifted her weight on the seat. "So after Taylor handed the money over to him, the middleman led the girls and Taylor and Marilee on quite a chase through the countryside." She chuckled. "I have quite a Keystone Kops image of that. And he finally drove up to his own home in Kilgore." They all stared at her, appearing confused, so she told them the rest of her news in a stern voice. "Anyway, for the plan to work, we have to keep it secret until the real villain picks up the money here tomorrow morning. Not a word until then. Understand?"

They all nodded solemnly, but would they take her advice? After all, gossip was one of the nursing home's most precious commodities, and it was how they had all come to know one another as victims of the same type of crime. It wouldn't be easy for them to keep such an interesting turn of events to themselves. She shrugged and stood up. "It's getting late. Why don't we let Camille have her room back and all of us try to get some sleep."

Although it was clear to Edith that most likely none of them would have an easy time following her directions, they all quietly began to move toward the door. Helped by her rollator, she walked over to Camille's bedside and leaned close to her ear. "Should I turn the light out as I leave, Camille?"

"Sure." Camille yawned. "Good night, and thanks for everything. I won't say a word."

❖

After everyone finished their dinner, which didn't take long, Elise yawned. "It's getting late. I better get back to my colleague's house. The city hall official may contact him. Thanks for all your work, and I'll see you at Silverado tomorrow morning. Zooey and Gloria, please go straight home. Don't get into trouble at this point."

After Elise left and the others were gathering purses and keys for their departure, Gloria spoke up. "Elise gave us good advice. I'd like to go home now, if you don't mind, but I'd love to ride in the Ghia once more, if that's all right with you, Miss Taylor."

"That's just fine, Gloria. Zooey, we'll see you back in the driveway at Bradford's Arbor in about twenty minutes. Okay?"

Zooey nodded, obviously disappointed by the short time limit. "But at least we'll have one more ride in that car!"

As the girls drove away, Taylor smiled at Marilee. "I'm sure they wanted to stop by the Dairy Queen in the Ghia, but I'm more than ready for this day to be over."

❖

A few minutes later, Elise parked. She could see the house in Kilgore, but it would take a major effort to spot her. She settled back in her seat and dialed her task-force colleague.

In a few minutes, he was knocking on the car window. She sat up and unlocked the doors. "Hop in, Corporal Broderick," Elise said. "You've had quite a night, haven't you, Buddy? You handled the chase very well, under the circumstances."

"Well, it would have been better if I'd known those juvenile delinquents were waiting for me."

"That's on me," Elise said. "I'd asked that the situation with the Silverado hoaxes stay separate from our fraud investigation at city hall. I didn't know you'd be the bag man at Silverado. And I sure didn't know they would try to tail you!"

He frowned and chewed his gum double-time. "The plan was for us to meet at Silverado for the handover in the morning. But he must have gotten a burr under his saddle, because he showed up here at my house about half an hour ago, demanding I hand over the money immediately."

"Any idea why he decided to pick up the money early? Did he say anything at all?"

Buddy shrugged. "He said something about a tip-off from his contact at Silverado. Any idea what that means?"

"I'm afraid I might." Elise swallowed hard. "The leader of the gals that call themselves Senior Sleuths told a resident that her grandson was unharmed and uninvolved in this money grab. But she swore them all to secrecy."

"Great idea. Swear them to secrecy. How could that fail?" Buddy sneered.

"What's to keep him from leaving town tonight with the money?" Elise asked.

Buddy wiped a hand across his face, smiling faintly. "For what it's worth, I switched out most of the money for fake bills as soon as I got home this evening. I know we'd prefer to catch him with the whole amount, so I built in a little delay. I told him I suspected that some of the payoff was counterfeit and invited him to count it with me. When he snapped that he'd been shortchanged, he was all for charging back to Silverado. But I persuaded him that going there tomorrow morning would arouse less suspicion. He took the bag, and its mixture of real and fake money, with him, determined to get the rest of the payoff tomorrow."

Elise beamed at him. "We have time to get ready for him at Silverado in the morning. He'll be coming for Camille to get the rest of the money. Does he have any idea how close we are to proving his involvement in insurance fraud, too?"

"No. I hope not."

"Okay, good. I got a tip from the girls this evening that may help us wrap up that part of the investigation soon, too. I'll work on that now and plan to meet you at Silverado at first light," Elise said. "Hope you can get a little sleep. See you soon."

CHAPTER XVIII

Showdown at Silverado

Marilee had expected to find the Silverado dining room empty of all but the earliest risers, but to her surprise, the room was at least half full. A buzz of conversation greeted her as she and Taylor arrived promptly at seven a.m. She whispered to Taylor, "What do you make of all these people being here?"

"A security leak," Taylor hissed. "I bet every one of these residents has heard what went on in Kilgore yesterday, and they don't want to miss a minute of whatever happens next."

Marilee spotted Edith and led the way to her table, where Camille also sat, propped up in her wheelchair. "Hey, you two. How's it going this morning? What brings half of Silverado to the breakfast table so early?"

Edith gestured to the next table, where Mrs. Richards, Mr. Yandle, and Mrs. Gray sat, visibly leaning in the direction of Edith's table. "Remember the phrase 'loose lips sink ships,' from the war? Although we were all sworn to secrecy about the money paid to supposedly help Camille's grandson, clearly we have many loose lips and a few sunken ships around here. But you can't really blame any of us. This mess affects us all. We're a tight-knit community, and we all deserve to know how everything turns out."

Just then Sergeant Elise Mora and Corporal Buddy Broderick

stepped through the double doors from the kitchen and stopped. Elise made a shushing gesture and spoke so that only those who had breakfast without their hearing aids missed what she said.

"Please, everyone." After introducing herself and her fellow officer, she announced, "Corporal Broderick—that's Buddy here—and I need your help. We believe that soon we will be arresting some folks who have been behind some misery at Silverado." She addressed everyone in the dining room. "We don't have time to send you to your rooms. So please remain as calm as you can and try to remember anything that happens as accurately as possible. You could be asked to testify in court."

Buddy spoke up next. "The one who's been extorting money from some of you may be arriving any minute. Please don't try to help us. We have your safety uppermost in our minds, so we plan to get him away from the dining room. But that might take a minute. So, again, please stay quiet and calm. We'll be right behind these doors, but we need to stay out of sight as long as possible."

Elise and Buddy retreated behind the kitchen doors, and the room fell quiet for a whole minute. A buzz of conversation was just beginning to build again when a tall man appeared at the front of the room, his arm around Miss Davis. "Shut up!" he yelled. Miss Davis attempted to speak, and he clamped a hand over her mouth. As the room quieted, her struggles to get away from him subsided. He turned to the room with a snarl. "Which one of you is Camille?"

With a burst of fear, Marilee saw Taylor immediately stand up. *Oh, please, don't be a hero just now*, she begged silently. But as she watched, Taylor achieved her full height, which, though not imposing, radiated a strength and authority that clearly calmed the residents.

The tall man spoke to Taylor, who stood near him. "Hand over the rest of what you owe me, and everybody will be okay."

Miss Davis struggled to speak, but Taylor cut her off. "I don't have the money. I turned it over to your accomplice at six o'clock last night. That's the last I know about it. If one of your own henchmen has double-crossed you, you'll have to suffer the consequences. But I insist that we have this conversation elsewhere."

Miss Davis found her voice. "This man is Assistant City Manager Ralph Peterson. For the past year he's been blackmailing me."

"Shut up, you hag!" Peterson shouted. "You didn't need blackmailing. You came to me suggesting how to maximize profits at this city-managed facility."

Miss Davis turned to him, radiating fury. "You greedy fool. I merely wanted to alert you that some Silverado residents could afford to pay more than others. And then you threatened my dogs! I had to go along with your scheme or lose the dearest things in my life."

"Those dogs would be better off dead, you old coot!"

With gratitude, Marilee saw that Taylor was beginning to speak. "Let's calm down. Lower your voices, both of you," Taylor said. "In fact, why don't you two sit at that empty table at the entrance. I'll come sit with you, and we'll try to make sense of this." Taylor began walking toward them, and Miss Davis plopped down abruptly at the table indicated. Assistant City Manager Peterson appeared confused but sat, too.

Taylor spoke sternly to them. "You two are finished. Your best course would be to tell your story to the police and accept the punishment you deserve. Will you be able to make restitution to the other victims from Silverado, Mr. Peterson? That would certainly help your case."

From her position in the middle of the room, Marilee could see that Taylor had convinced Miss Davis and Mr. Peterson to sit down. But even with her hearing aids, she couldn't make out everything they were saying. She hoped Elise and Buddy would come out of the kitchen, where they'd disappeared to, but she saw no sign of them. She glanced at Dr. Edith, who appeared to be studying Camille's face for signs of stress. Marilee could see confusion all around her, but few signs of fear or anger on the residents' faces. *Maybe this will be okay.*

But just then, Miss Davis screamed at peak volume. "Let go of me, you brute." All eyes turned to the three at the front table. Miss Davis clenched her right hand into a fist.

Taylor's jaw tensed, her blue eyes blazing. "Miss Davis, please keep your voice down. Mr. Peterson, please keep your hands to yourself. Adding assault to your list of offenses won't help your case," Taylor said.

"She was trying to take my stun gun." Peterson moaned. "It's the only defense I have against all you old crows."

A ripple of laughter swept through the dining room as the old crows apparently heard his slur. Clearly, they were not about to let this coward intimidate them. Marilee was relieved when Taylor spoke. "We have a criminal and his colleague with us, so remaining quiet and calm is the best way to care for ourselves. Miss Davis, since you're one of Silverado's own, would you care to explain your role in what's been going on here?"

Marilee was relieved to see Miss Davis lean away from Peterson and toward Taylor, perhaps realigning her loyalties? Miss Davis's motive became clearer as she spoke. "I have been friends with many of you for some time. In fact, a few of you may remember my beloved dog Suzie, who died last year. I haven't been the same since. I still have my baby boy Laddy, but that's only because I've had to go along with this miserable snake. He killed Suzie to force me to help him with his plan to extort money from Silverado residents."

The group gasped audibly in clear disbelief, and Marilee noticed a few residents wiping tears from their eyes. Miss Davis's voice had faltered when she mentioned Suzie's death, but it gathered strength as she picked up her story. "Yes. That's right. One night about a year ago, I found Suzie dead on my back porch. Not far away was a nearly completely eaten hunk of steak with pieces of a white pill still clinging to it. I never fed Suzie or Laddy beef! I always boiled their chicken myself and carefully deboned it to be sure they wouldn't be injured. Instantly I knew who had done this heartless deed."

Miss Davis turned in her chair to face the man. "Ralph Peterson, who is now New Eden's assistant city manager, was once the cutest little boy you ever saw. The son of my upstairs neighbor, Ralph was a pleasant enough child until one day I caught him kicking my dog. He was little, maybe a first or second grader, so I felt obliged to take him to his mother for discipline. I marched him up the stairs and knocked on her door. And when she didn't answer immediately, I knocked again and heard a croak from within their apartment. Although Ralph was struggling to get away, I held his arm firmly until his mother opened the door a crack."

Ralph, who had covered one arm with his other hand, most likely was remembering the grip Miss Davis had held him with all those years ago. Marilee returned her attention to Miss Davis, who continued to tell her tale with obvious self-righteous pride.

"I could tell right away that his mother had been drinking, but I felt strongly that I couldn't ignore the abuse of an animal, so I told her the story through the partially open door. When I finished describing how I saw her son kick my dear fur buddy, I gently pushed him toward his mother and turned to go back to my apartment downstairs."

"Gently, my foot," Peterson said. "My arm still hurts where you gripped it and then shoved me through the door. And another part of me remembers how hard Mom whopped me when I got inside. But that was only the start of a very unneighborly relationship." He glared at her. "We couldn't afford to move, and I guess Devil Davis couldn't either, because she was always there, watching my every move, telling on me to Mom, and then later gossiping about me with some of my teachers. I never got a break."

"You didn't deserve a break, Ralph. You deserved a broken neck. After the kicking incident, I had to make sure you weren't around when I let my dear doggies out, and on the rare occasion when they'd been out of my sight, I had to inspect them carefully for evidence of further abuse from you. This went on for months, until your mom dropped dead of alcoholism and you were sent off to the state home."

"As a matter of fact, that was the only good thing that happened to me," Ralph said. "I finally found a stable living situation, and by attending a different school, I escaped the reputation you helped build for me. I graduated from high school, went to college, and landed a good job in the city manager's office here. My life was going pretty good until you showed up at city hall. That stupid dog, your death grip on my arm, your never-ending tattling to anyone who would listen—it all came back. In spite of that, your con sounded very interesting."

Marilee allowed herself a slight shift in position so she could see whether Elise was still in the kitchen and able to hear what was going on. Through a crack between the swinging doors she glimpsed Elise, who made a "keep them talking" gesture with her hand so that only those at the back of the dining room could have seen it. Of course nobody was paying any attention to the kitchen area. They were all focused on Miss Davis and Mr. Peterson at the front. Obviously, Taylor understood the situation, being aware that they had many witnesses to what was clearly developing into a confession.

Marilee realized that Camille was beginning to speak as she labored to stand up. "I'm glad you are all feeling so at home. But you have made me anything but comfortable for the last several days. I want you two to tell me why you picked my grandson a your target."

Miss Davis spoke up. "Your grandson wasn't the target, dear. *You* were. This lowlife here has been forcing me to turn over financial records of Silverado residents whose assets are significant enough to yield a considerable sum in ransom money. He started small with Mrs. Richards. Then he upped the ante with Mr. Yandle and Mrs. Gray. You arrived only recently, and although your medical picture wasn't great and your bank account didn't appear very healthy, I was finally able to determine that your financial guarantor was very well off indeed. That made you an excellent target. And everything was going perfectly well until those brats from the high school started working at Silverado."

Edith spoke up from her table in the middle of the room. "Miss Davis, I happen to know both of those young women, and they have brought significant changes to our lives. Zooey is so much fun when she comes to visit. And Gloria obviously has a real head for business. She and that young man who works with the computers in the basement have really begun to make a difference in how quickly our issues with insurance companies are being dealt with. They've both contributed marvelous things to our lives at Silverado."

Peterson ignored Edith. Instead, he snapped at Miss Davis. "Keep your trap shut, you old biddy! You'll land us both in prison."

And then Miss Davis stopped, perhaps realizing that her insights were self-incriminating, even though they made clear the role that Peterson had played in the crimes. Miss Davis and Mr. Peterson both lapsed into silence.

Camille hadn't finished. Holding on to the back of a chair for support, she started interrogating Davis and Peterson. "Do you have any idea the torment you've put all of us through? It wasn't until some of my friends noticed I'd withdrawn and wasn't coming to the dining room for meals that I learned I wasn't the only one who'd had a relative threatened with jail time unless they paid ransom." She put one hand over her heart briefly. "And you really hurt me by somehow making it sound like my grandson was really, truly the one on the phone, begging me to pay up." A sob caught in her throat. "Now, that was cruel. Money is just money, but making me fear for my only grandbaby's life, even for just a moment, is horrible."

Marilee caught Edith's worried expression. She could tell that Edith was concerned about Camille's medical condition, and she remembered the lingering emotional effect of Camille's family rupture. Thank God Taylor had jumped in to take the brunt of Peterson's rage. Who knew how much more Camille could stand? The physician in Edith was obviously not pleased by the way this morning's events were affecting her friend.

Edith took Camille's hand, speaking to her softly. "Sit down, dear. You mustn't upset yourself. I know you remember what your doctor told you about keeping stress to a minimum."

Camille nodded at Edith and began the slow process of sitting back down. "Of course I remember, but surely you can't begrudge me a chance to confront the swine who've caused so much misery."

Suddenly Peterson jumped up and shouted, "Shut up, all of you," reclaiming the attention of everyone in the room. "You're about to make me forget why I'm here. I want my money! As soon as I get it, I'll leave and let you get back to your sad little lives. If I don't get it, you'll all be glad to see the end of our beloved Miss Davis right here in the Silverado dining room."

Taylor shot up from her chair. "No, sir. We're not having that. Murder is not on the menu here at Silverado, Mr. Peterson. As far as I know, I handed over a bag containing a good bit of cash to someone acting as your agent yesterday. You know what they say about honor among thieves. Did your own bag man trick you?"

Peterson paled but stood his ground. "You mean to say that the bag you gave him really did contain the money in used twenties as I specified?"

"I am an officer of the court, sir. And I don't trifle where money is concerned. I am sorry to tell you that I followed your instructions. Someone else must have double-crossed you. In fact, I would urge you to acknowledge that you have no further business with anyone here at Silverado. You should find the one who picked up the money. In any event, it's time for you to leave."

Taylor's bluster was apparently working. Marilee saw Peterson glance away from Taylor, past Miss Davis, and toward the exit. Maybe he would just walk out.

But it wasn't over yet. Mr. Yandle had stood and was helping Mrs. Gray to her feet. "Stop right there," Yandle said, his voice quavering. "You owe me personally some ten thousand dollars, which I need if I am to afford staying in this lovely facility. So you're not going anywhere until I have my money back."

"Me, too," whispered Mrs. Gray, whose coloring had begun to match her name. Seated beside Mrs. Richards, Mrs. Gray was pushing on the table in front of her to be able to stand but was clearly paying a high cost for that effort.

Dr. Edith got to her feet and gestured to Marilee to come help her. "Let's get these four out of here and back to their rooms."

"Sure," Marilee said, jumping up as quickly as she could manage and moving to help Camille take the brake off her wheelchair so she could be rolled to her room.

With her arms wide open, Edith was making encouraging sounds while trying to shepherd the three other hoax victims at the next table out of the room.

"This has got to stop," Peterson shouted, sounding desperate. "Everybody sit back down. No one is leaving this dining room until I have my money."

"You have my money, you dirt bag," Mr. Yandle said, more than a little short of breath.

"That's right," Miss Davis said, "and I suspect I know where he keeps it."

Marilee recognized the expression on Taylor's face. It was her *this is the last straw* expression, which became evident when she was on the phone with customer service for her computer. Fearing the Silverado dining room was about to explode into senior-modulated chaos, Marilee whispered to Camille to sit tight and turned her full attention to the double doors to the kitchen. With her hands folded in supplication, she said to the apparently disinterested doors, "Now, please."

CHAPTER XIX

Culprits Arrested

Suddenly the white kitchen doors swung apart, and out stepped Sergeant Elise Mora and Corporal Buddy Broderick, holding their service revolvers in front of them. Everyone in the dining area, including Taylor, froze in place. Many thrust their arms into the air as if they'd been caught in the act. Some of the old people shook from head to toe, others glanced around the room randomly, a few scowled, and one frail-appearing woman slumped to the faux wood plank floor in a faint.

However, a few opened their eyes wide and even grinned as they watched Sergeant Mora take control. As an aide dashed over to care for the woman who lay on the floor, Taylor knew that everyone here would remember this breakfast for a long time to come.

Just then, Miss Davis and Mr. Peterson glanced at each other and darted toward the doors like a couple of children avoiding a come-to-supper whistle.

But before they could make a getaway, a new voice blasted through the large room. "Stop right there, sir," someone commanded. "You've already broken the law. Don't make it any harder on yourself than it already is. We are from the Federal Task Force on Elder Abuse based in Dallas. You are both under arrest."

Not recognizing this new addition to their early morning breakfast with the bad guys, the residents stared at the newcomers. A large, uniformed man and a slim woman in civilian clothes stood at the entrance to the dining area. The two radiated confidence.

The residents continued to sit on the edge of their dining chairs, many with their hands still in the air. Silence filled the room, broken occasionally by various gasps, coughs, sneezes, and sighs. The two newcomers approached Miss Davis and Mr. Peterson, who appeared to instinctively cringe and shrink in the law enforcement duo's presence.

Peterson, perspiration shining on his forehead from the sun's rays pouring through the room's windows, clutched his small stun gun in his raised hand. However, his shaking arm appeared to be losing its strength, his long fingers loosening and the weapon almost melting from his grip, though he didn't drop it. The uniformed newcomer strode up to Peterson and effortlessly took it from his limp hand, then pocketed it.

"Good move, sir," the new officer said. "At least we won't have to add resisting arrest to the list of charges we've assembled so far."

Likewise, the female officer stood before Miss Davis, placing a hand firmly on her shoulder. At the stranger's touch, Miss Davis almost seemed to dissolve like the Wicked Witch of the West, her head drooping as she let the woman guide her to the uniformed local officers.

"As commanders of the Dallas-based Federal Task Force on Elder Abuse, we are informing you that you are under arrest. At the local police station, you will be informed of your rights and of the charges pending against you," the woman said firmly to both the prisoners. "It is in your best interests to cooperate fully."

Peterson glanced around the dining hall, filled with gaping senior citizens, as if he were considering a move from an action movie, but with the two local officers manning the swinging kitchen doors, and the newly arrived authorities dominating the front entrance, he meekly let the large officer cuff him.

Miss Davis also surveyed the familiar room, filled with the people whose personal information she was privy to, as if begging them to help her avoid the inevitable. But she deflated like a leaking balloon, letting the officers take her into custody, too.

Taylor almost felt sorry for her. Who would care for her beloved dog if she received a prison sentence? Yet she then recalled Miss Davis's faithful assistant. She would undoubtedly support her boss during the difficult times ahead. However unpleasant Miss Davis might be, she had her good points. Even Peterson was a victim of sorts, given his poor parenting, though he would probably receive a much harsher sentence than Miss Davis would.

As the tension of the arrest began to ease, and several attendants had revived the fallen residents, Zooey and Gloria were allowed through the kitchen doors. "We came by really early to see what would happen because we're driving to Dallas this weekend with Zooey's mom," Gloria told Taylor.

"What did we miss?" Zooey was staring around the dining hall. "We've been waiting forever for them to let us in because of a disturbance, as they're calling it out front." She frowned. "And why are so many people in here this early? This place is usually like a morgue until about eight thirty."

"Well, thanks to a total lack of confidentiality, a whole lot of us have just witnessed confessions to not one but two nursing home hoaxes," Taylor told them.

"What? You did? What happened?" Zooey asked. "Tell us!"

The girls kept glancing around until Gloria pointed at the woman she'd worked for. "Why does Miss Davis have on handcuffs? Is she the one who's been stealing from these old people?"

"She's an accessory to the crimes," Taylor said, "so I doubt she'll be employed here or anywhere else, at least for a while. We'll leave that decision up to the courts."

"So if she's not the one to blame, who's the main bad guy?" Zooey asked, then paused.

"The bad guy you asked about is the assistant city manager, Ralph Peterson. The man whose office you peeked into at city hall. He may be in a lot more trouble than he bargained for."

Marilee and Edith walked up just then. "Hi, Zooey, Gloria. Sorry you missed all the excitement," Marilee said. "None of us had any idea there would be so much drama this early." She rolled her eyes.

"I just wanted to touch base with all of you before I walk Camille back to her room." Edith glanced over to where her friend sat quietly, as if in a daze. "She's decided to have her breakfast brought to her in an hour or so, after she's had a chance to settle down and recover from all this excitement. And I'll probably join her."

"That might be a good idea for several of the people in this group," Taylor said, "though I suspect some of these folks will probably eat more than they usually do. Events like this can work up a good appetite." She touched her stomach. "Mine included."

"May I have a word with you?" The female officer who had been part of the arrest of the two scoundrels had just walked up to their little group. "My partner, who's corralling the lawbreakers over there, and I are leading a federal task force on elder abuse. We were investigating insurance fraud at Silverado, but Sergeant Mora told us about your efforts to stop the hoaxes involving Silverado residents."

Taylor held out her hand. "I'm glad to meet you, Officer. Sergeant Mora has done an excellent job with both types of elder abuse here at Silverado."

The officer shook Taylor's hand. "Sergeant Mora has kept us apprised about the developments in this case. Just this morning we had a breakthrough, thanks to a tip from members of your team. We're a little late getting to the dining room because of the gold mine of information about insurance fraud the guy in the basement turned over to us."

As she spoke, she waved at a young man who'd just come into the dining room from the kitchen. "Hi, John. I'm talking about you. Pull up a chair.

"John here used his hacking skills a couple of years ago to get even with some high school bullies, but the judge probated his sentence on the condition that he find work that would employ his technical skills in a positive way. He chose a job at Silverado as a tribute to his deceased grandparents. He thought he would be able to streamline reporting to Medicaid and Medicare, and he did. But he also uncovered some very suspicious discrepancies in reporting medical procedures performed on residents. He just wasn't sure who to tell, so he was glad to hear from Elise last night. They spent several hours going over the evidence he'd accumulated."

Taylor looked toward John with gratitude and started to speak, but the commander hadn't finished.

"I've been authorized to offer Sergeant Mora a leadership position on our task force in Dallas."

Marilee beamed. "What a great idea. I bet she'll jump at the chance. Won't you, Elise? She'll be an amazing addition to your team, Commander."

"We'd like to commend the five of you as well," she said, gazing at Taylor, Marilee, Edith, Zooey, and Gloria in turn. "We understand that you have all worked to solve these crimes against senior citizens, and we thank you for your outstanding service. But I have to add that before your next case, you should make time to take our undercover surveillance module."

Zooey and Gloria beamed, while the rest of them nodded, aware of the rebuke hidden in the praise.

"Thank you for your expression of gratitude," Taylor said. "We're definitely amateurs, but it has been a real pleasure to do what we can to help make life easier for people we know and love in our small town."

"We'll be in touch about this case," the woman said. "In the meantime, have a pleasant day, and keep up the good work."

As the task force commander turned to her partner and the two criminals, Zooey said, "Wow. Wait till I tell everybody that she thanked us like we did something extra special. I don't imagine that happens to many people around here, do you, Glo?"

Gloria appeared dazed by the entire incident at the nursing home. "I doubt it. We're really lucky to get to do something important like this." She took a deep breath. "And it wasn't too hard, was it? To be honest, it was fun, and I learned a lot about the real world."

"But, more important," Zooey said, staring down at the floor, "I don't guess you'll need me to drive your Karmann Ghia anymore, now that this case is solved." Her eyes dulled.

"As for my Karmann Ghia…" Taylor almost laughed aloud at Zooey's obvious distress about the car, "I imagine I could let you take it out on a few special occasions, if you promise to drive really carefully."

Zooey threw her arms around Taylor and gave her a big hug. "I will! Thank you, thank you, thank you. All my friends will be so jealous, won't they, Glo? I can't wait to see their faces."

"Definitely. Especially if it involves driving the Karmann Ghia." They all chuckled.

"Well, we better hit the road. Mom wants to get to Dallas as soon as we can."

"Sure thing," Taylor said. "Have a great weekend."

After the girls left and the criminals had been led away, Marilee said to Elise, Taylor, and Edith, "I'm thirsty after all this excitement. Could we maybe get something to drink?"

Taylor surveyed the recently emptied dining room. "I don't see why not. Let me ask in the kitchen."

She soon returned holding glasses on a tray, and they strolled over to stand beside the shiny grand piano that dominated the entertainment area. "Shall we toast the successful conclusion of our first Senior Sleuths case? It's been quite an experience, hasn't it? I feel sure Nancy Drew would approve."

"Nancy Drew?" Elise asked. "Did you read those novels? She was a role model for me."

"Every last one of them. When I was a girl, I always asked for the latest one as a birthday or Christmas present," Taylor said. "They had blue covers with the black figure of a slim girl holding a magnifying glass. In fact, I may still have a few of them on my bookshelves."

"What about you, Edith? Did you read them, too? I certainly did," Marilee said.

"Yes, and Cherry Ames, and Penny Parker." She smiled. "And I can't speak for all young Black girls like me, but I found them so exciting I almost didn't care that Nancy had blond hair and blue eyes. I always got so caught up in her adventures and her independence and her self-confidence that it didn't matter what she looked like. I just wanted to be like her."

"Hear, hear," Marilee said. "I'll drink to that. And, as old as I am, I still want to be like Nancy, too."

CHAPTER XX

Celebration

Over a muesli breakfast a few days later, Taylor said, "I've begun to feel a little restless. What's next?"

"Funny you should ask." Marilee put her spoon down. "I've been talking to Edith about her being released from in-house rehab. Shouldn't we celebrate our victory over the forces of evil in that hoax at the nursing home? Edith really wants an excuse to make her very special groundnut stew, and I bet our kitchen at Bradford's Arbor, with a little help from your private chef, would be the perfect place to prepare the feast. We could invite the whole gang from Silverado, plus our law enforcement buddies and your Lois and her mom. The girls, too, of course. This could be a grand occasion."

Taylor shouted, "Sounds great! And it provides just the excuse I've been needing to brighten up the living and dining rooms. I'm ready for a new era at Bradford's Arbor. Let's ask Lois to help us see how pretty those rooms are without the gloom of heavy drapes." Taylor stood up. "Now that it's summertime, I'm ready to let in the sun and acknowledge that my life has more light in it than it has in years. And it's all thanks to you, my dear senior sleuth."

Taylor pulled Marilee up from her chair, hugged her close, and skipped off to the office to ask Lois to help with the curtains.

Marilee watched Taylor leave. *Light. That's what we do need. Removing the drapes will help, and having a new purpose in life will brighten our days.*

"Lois said we can get by with sheers in the living and dining rooms," Taylor said as she waltzed through the kitchen a few minutes later, carrying the dark, heavy drapery that had blocked out daylight in the Arbor's main rooms. "I'll bet Daddy chose drapes like these after Mother died, probably trying to keep the world at bay, and I've just quit replacing them. Could you get the back door for me, Marilee? I'm on my way to the dumpster with these dusty old things. And if you want to help, you can get the ones in the dining room."

Marilee headed there—slowly, carefully.

❖

A week later, Bradford's Arbor appeared noticeably different. The heavy drapes had departed with Thursday's garbage pickup. New off-white sheers covered the windows. Sunlight filled both rooms.

Marilee and Taylor felt as though years of family history had stopped clouding their everyday existence and now resided in scrapbooks shelved for easy reference. They had commented to each other just that morning that they both felt lighter and happier, though Marilee had to admit that she still hadn't lost any weight. They were delighted to be working together to celebrate the successful conclusion of their first case as Senior Sleuths: The Nursing Home Hoax.

Edith had been released from Silverado two days earlier, with plans to continue her physical therapy on an outpatient basis. Having demonstrated that she could make the climb to her second-floor room, Edith moved into Bradford's Arbor. Taylor enlisted Zooey to drive them to do their shopping in Marilee's Rogue. She was clearly disappointed not to drive the Ghia, but everyone agreed it wasn't a good shopping cart. They'd mainly scoured the local grocery stores for the necessary ingredients for Edith's groundnut-stew recipe. Peanuts were the groundnuts in the stew, and they'd all been forced to scrutinize peanut-butter labels closely to find a brand with no sugar or salt added.

Taylor restaged the living room and supervised the cleaning of the dining room carpet, which, once inspected in better light, seriously needed a shampoo.

When the successful shoppers had unloaded their purchases in the Arbor's kitchen, Zooey announced that she had a summer school class to attend and waved good-bye. The Arbor's chef, Greta, nodded at everyone while eyeing the recipe carefully. "This calls for a lot of garlic and ginger. Are you sure about that, Dr. Edith?"

"Definitely. In West Africa we use lots of garlic and ginger to keep us healthy."

Having heard Dr. Edith's explanation, Greta began chopping vigorously.

Lois's grandmother, June, was curious, too, and joined the kitchen crew to cut up the collards and kale for the stew. "This recipe's new to me, though it surely contains lots of familiar ingredients. But why doesn't it have any meat in it?"

"This recipe comes from the area where I had my clinic, outside Kumasi in Ghana, West Africa," Edith said. "But I grew up in East Texas, too. And it's pretty clear there's a link between the cuisine of West Africa and the food prepared by their descendants in the American South. Also, when it comes to eating, East Texas is definitely part of the South. If we were in Ghana, we would probably put goat meat in the stew, but I've long preferred a vegetarian diet. I suspect Taylor does, too."

"You're right about Miss Taylor," June said. "And my granddaughter Lois shares that preference with you and Taylor, Dr. Edith. On the other hand, Lois won't eat kale when I cook it for her, but I bet she'll like it in this recipe. I see it calls for sweet potatoes, but shouldn't it have some okra in it, Dr. Edith?"

"Well, okra's a controversial ingredient, even in West

Africa these days. Why don't we offer some fried okra as a side dish, rather than cook it in the stew? That way the folks who didn't grow up with cooked okra won't have a conniption fit over the slime that serves as an excellent thickening agent." Edith rubbed her hands together. "We'll also provide some chopped peanuts and chives. That reminds me. Do we have a large enough bowl to serve the stew to the crowd Taylor and Marilee have invited?"

"Absolutely," Greta replied. "This house has served many large groups, mainly back in Mr. Bradford's day, but occasionally hosted by Miss Taylor. We have a beautiful old soup tureen and plenty of bowls to go with it. What should we do with the brown rice? Put it in the bottom of the tureen or in a separate serving bowl?"

"If you're asking me," June said, "a separate bowl would definitely be better. Folks might miss the rice completely if it's at the bottom of the tureen, and if they're in the same bowl, those who never eat rice are sure to scoop some up."

"You're right, again," Edith said. "Separate bowls for the rice and the stew. We're making the stew today to serve tomorrow because the flavors need time to blend, but we'll cook the rice, fry the okra, and make the salad just before we serve them. You've agreed to fix the salad, right, Miss Marilee? That reminds me. Who's bringing dessert? I know somebody volunteered, but I can't remember who."

"Elise Mora, I believe Taylor said," Marilee answered. "She's the local police sergeant who'll soon be moving to Dallas to join the federal task force. I don't know exactly what she's bringing, but she wanted to do something, and dessert it is. My job is the salad, and I've got plenty of tomatoes and greens from our garden to make it really delicious." Marilee picked up an avocado. "Would be all right if I chopped a couple of these into the salad? Edith, what's your opinion?"

"The creaminess of the avocados will be a lovely complement

to the spicy soup. This is a celebration, and we don't want to leave anyone's culture out. Gloria's originally from Central America, isn't she?" Edith asked.

"You're right. El Salvador. I like your inclusive thinking," Marilee replied.

Just then, Taylor poked her head into the crowded kitchen. "Wow. It's busy in here. Everything going okay for tomorrow? It makes such a difference to have more light in the living-dining area. I can't wait to introduce our fresh surroundings to everybody. Do you need me to do anything?"

Marilee spoke for the group. "Please don't come in. It's crowded enough as it is. We don't need any more help. You and Lois keep on making everything look good out there. But do you know what Elise is bringing for dessert? We're curious about what she's making and the kind of serving dishes we'll need."

"I believe she said tres leches cake. Does that sound right?" Taylor replied.

"That sounds *great*," Marilee said. "Now run along. We've got things under control in here."

❖

The next afternoon, at about five o'clock, guests started arriving at Bradford's Arbor. With a little help from Barb and Shannon, the next-door neighbor and her friend, Taylor had put together a temporary ramp from the porte cochere into the glass-paned foyer. When the Silverado van pulled up, Taylor, Marilee, and Edith were there to assist where needed. Edith was eager to greet the friends who'd been through the hoaxes together.

First to come down the van's lift was Camille. Today she was clearly doing much better than she had been, her eyes bright above a pretty pink shirt and pants. Although still in a wheelchair, she was using her feet to speed up her ride. All three hosts greeted her warmly and made sure she got a glass of something cool as soon as she entered the foyer. Lois was there beside a tray of both iced tea and lemonade, to greet every guest with a beverage.

Following Camille were Mrs. Richards and Mrs. Gray. John, affectionately known as the geek in the basement, was there to help them get out. They both used walkers to help them get up the ramp, but Mr. Yandle proudly walked behind them, not needing any assistance at all. Marilee noticed that both women were bickering over who would hand him his glass of lemonade. The excitement around the hoax had evidently energized all three of them.

Finally, Gloria and the administrator of Silverado climbed out of the front of the van, though Marilee had never met the administrator during all the time she'd spent at the facility. Gloria stepped up to introduce her to the hostesses. "I'm not sure how many of you know Ms. Hurd. She's been away from the office a lot lately, dealing with health issues of her own."

Ms. Hurd spoke to them. "I owe you three a huge debt of gratitude. You've changed what could easily have been a disaster into a major victory in the effort to fight crimes against the elderly. I'm so sorry I couldn't be there to support your efforts, though you have done very well without me. But I've discovered that we can't do without Gloria. The order she brought to the assistant administrator's office was impressive," Ms. Hurd said. "As you doubtless expected, Miss Davis will no longer be working at Silverado, and her assistant has retired so she can devote herself to caring for Miss Davis's dog full-time.

"With two vacancies in that department, I've asked Gloria if she could work at least half-time. With John in the basement and Gloria upstairs, we hope to keep out of hot water with the various agencies to whom we report. And she'll be able to help her family with the bookkeeping at their new restaurant when it opens and take a course or two at the college, starting in the fall. I'm hoping she'll consider coming to work with us full-time at some point soon."

The assembled guests applauded Gloria, and just then the unmistakable sound of the Karmann Ghia pulling in behind the van interrupted them. Jerking the car lightly to a stop, Zooey hopped out and joined the clapping. Gloria spoke up. "Zooey deserves your applause, too. She brought a positive outlook to many Silverado residents, and I know they appreciated it."

"That's right!" Mr. Yandle shouted, leading the next round of applause for both Zooey and Gloria. Marilee noticed that the two older women had followed Yandle back outside, each of them holding out an extra glass of lemonade for him.

Gloria spoke up once more. "These two Senior Sleuths are the ones who deserve the most credit. They paid attention to what was going on and sent Zooey and me undercover to get the specifics about the situation at Silverado."

More applause greeted Taylor and Marilee, who'd joined Gloria and Zooey. Taylor spoke to the crowd gathered in the driveway. "We're all grateful for your support in solving our first case as Senior Sleuths. But I don't know what we're doing, standing outside in the afternoon heat. Come on inside, get yourself something to sip on, and I'll give you a tour of our newly brightened-up living and dining area."

As the guests made their way through the foyer into the redecorated living room, another car arrived in the driveway, where Edith and Marilee had lingered, hoping the dessert was on its way. After the new car pulled up, the driver got out and hurried to open his passenger's door. She handed him a large cake carrier before climbing out and reclaiming the box.

"Welcome, Sergeant Mora," Edith said. "Are you the bearer of our dessert?"

"I am! This is my mother's recipe for a tres leches cake. She insisted I make it for this celebration. You've probably all seen Corporal Broderick, but you may not have been introduced. Buddy, this is the doctor who helped tip us off to the AI scams at Silverado, and you've already met Marilee and Taylor."

"Yes. He has," Marilee said. "Elise, if you'll follow Edith to the kitchen, she'll help you find a place to put that cake carrier until it's time to serve dessert. Buddy, if you'll step into the foyer, Lois will have a glass of something for you. If you hurry, you can catch the tour Taylor's offering."

Marilee lingered on the lawn, taking in the huge magnolia tree in the afternoon light. The heat of the day fell around her like a warm embrace, and for the first time, she felt that Bradford's Arbor might truly be her home. When she remembered that the salad was waiting for her to assemble, she took a final look around and hurried to the back of the house to enter the kitchen.

❖

Half an hour later, Taylor struck her crystal lemonade glass with a spoon. "It's time to eat, friends. But first, I'd like to ask Dr. Edith to tell us a little about the groundnut stew she's orchestrated for us as part of our celebration."

Dr. Edith stood. "As some of you know, I lived in West Africa for almost sixty years, but I was an East Texan before that. For me, this is a homecoming, and if I were welcoming you to my home outside Kumasi in Ghana, I would serve you groundnut stew. It's a celebratory dish, offered to guests and for special occasions." She cleared her throat. "This is surely a special occasion."

The guests murmured their agreement, and Dr. Edith continued. "The dish goes by many names because so many languages are spoken in West Africa, where peanuts—yes, we call them groundnuts—are a common crop. And everyone gives it a special name in their own language. Typically, the stew is prepared with meat, but we have a vegetarian version for you tonight." Several of the guests nodded their appreciation. "The base is vegetable broth with tomato paste, flavored with garlic and fresh ginger, sugar- and salt-free peanut butter, chopped greens, and sweet potatoes. It's served with brown rice and side dishes of chopped peanuts, chives, and fried okra—for those of you who want to add even more flavor."

Edith turned in Taylor's direction. "I know you don't usually eat hot stews in the summer in Texas, so I've asked Taylor to adjust the air conditioning to keep you comfortable. We've also included a salad of fresh greens and vegetables from the garden here at Bradford's Arbor. For dessert, Miss Elise has made her mother's tres leches cake, and the supply of tea and lemonade is endless."

With that, the guests began applauding and moving toward the buffet laid out on the dining table. But Edith hadn't finished and raised her arms. "Sorry if you're ready to eat, but I almost forgot two important things, starting with the team that prepared this meal: the Arbor's own excellent chef, Greta; our housekeeper emerita, June; Lois, her granddaughter and Miss Taylor's assistant; as well as Miss Elise, who made the dessert, and Miss Marilee, who made the salad. The last thing—and, yes, Mr. Yandle, we plan to eat right away—is for me to say what a pleasure it is to have been asked to join the Senior Sleuth team. I have told my children they'll need to visit me here rather than in Ghana. I'm ready to stay in the land of my birth, to make whatever contributions I can to the health and welfare of my friends and neighbors in East Texas. And so, with a word of appreciation to the Almighty who brings us the food that we eat, let me get out of your way as you help yourselves to our celebration in a bowl: groundnut stew."

With that, Edith joined Taylor and Marilee, and they all stepped into the living room to allow their hungry guests easy access to the buffet. While there, she took the hands of her two longtime friends. "Thank you both for welcoming me into this new phase of my life. We've been on our paths for a long time, and finding that we can add new adventures together at our age is a wonderful discovery."

Still holding hands with Edith and Marilee, Taylor smiled into each pair of eyes in turn. "I can't imagine a more exhilarating way for us to enter our ninth decade than together, doing work that we relish, as friends and partners."

Marilee squeezed their hands tighter and started to speak. When tears filled her eyes, she closed her mouth and turned instead to plant a kiss on Edith's and then on Taylor's cheek.

About the Authors

Shelley Thrasher—former English professor and longtime BSB editor and author—and Ann Faulkner—former community college educator and staff-development facilitator—have teamed up to celebrate life after eighty.

Both native Texans, they enjoy traveling at home and abroad, reading and writing, eating out, having friends of all ages, giggling a lot, and cooking together—Ann's cat Mina adding spice to their efforts.
This is their first cozy mystery, and they hope it isn't their last.

Books Available From Bold Strokes Books

A Thousand Tiny Promises by Morgan Lee Miller. When estranged childhood friends Audrey and Reid reunite to fulfill their best friend's dying wish, the last thing they expect is a journey toward healing their broken friendship and discovering a newfound love for each other. (978-1-63679-630-7)

Behold My Heart by Ronica Black. Alora Anders is a highly successful artist who's losing her vision. Devastated, she hires Bodie Banks, a young struggling sculptor, as a live-in assistant. Can Alora open her mind and her heart to accept Bodie into her life? (978-1-63679-810-3)

Fearless Hearts by Radclyffe. One wounded woman, one determined to protect her—and a summertime of risk, danger, and desire. (978-1-63679-837-0)

Stranger in the Sand by Renee Roman. Grace Langley is haunted by guilt. Fagan Shaw wishes she could remember her past. Will finding each other bring the closure they're looking for in order to have a brighter future? (978-1-63679-802-8)

The Nursing Home Hoax by Shelley Thrasher and Ann Faulkner. In this fresh take for grown-ups on the classic Nancy Drew series, crime-solving duo Taylor and Marilee investigate suspicious activity at a small East Texas nursing home. (978-1-63679-806-6)

The Rise and Fall of Conner Cody by Chelsey Lynford. A successful yet lonely Hollywood starlet must decide if she can let go of old wounds and accept a chance at family, friendship, and the love of a lifetime. (978-1-63679-739-7)

A Conflict of Interest by Morgan Adams. Tensions rise when a one-night stand becomes a major conflict of interest between an up-and-coming senior associate and a dedicated cardiac surgeon. (978-1-63679-870-7)

A Magnificent Disturbance by Lee Lynch. These everyday dykes and their friends will stop at nothing to see the women's clinic thrive and, in the process, their ideals, their wounds, and a steadfast allegiance to one another make them heroes. (978-1-63679-031-2)

Big Corpse on Campus by Karis Walsh. When University Police Officer Cappy Flannery investigates what looks like a clear-cut suicide, she discovers that the case—and her feelings for librarian Jazz—are more complicated than she expected. (978-1-63679-852-3)

Charity Case by Jean Copeland. Bad girl Lindsay Chase came home to Connecticut for a fresh start, but an old, risky habit provides the chance to save the day for her new love, Ellie. (978-1-63679-593-5)

Moments to Treasure by Ali Vali. Levi Montbard and Yasmine Hassani have found a vast Templar treasure, but there is much more to the story—and what is left to be found. (978-1-63679-473-0)

The Stolen Girl by Cari Hunter. Detective Inspector Jo Shaw is determined to prove she's fit for work after an injury that almost killed her, but a new case brings her up against people who will do anything to preserve their own interests, putting Jo—and those closest to her—directly in the line of fire. (978-1-63679-822-6)

Discovering Gold by Sam Ledel. In 1920s Colorado, a single mother and a rowdy cowgirl must set aside their fears and initial reservations about one another if they want to find love in the mining town each of them calls home. (978-1-63679-786-1)

Dream a Little Dream by Melissa Brayden. Savanna can't believe it when Dr. Kyle Remington, the woman who left her feeling like a fool, shows up in Dreamer's Bay. Life is too complicated for second chances. Or is it? (978-1-63679-839-4)

Goodbye Hello by Heather K O'Malley. With so much time apart and the challenges of a long-distance relationship, Kelly and Teresa's second chance at love may end just as awkwardly as the first. (978-1-63679-790-8)

Emma by the Sea by Sarah G. Levine. A delightful modern-day romance inspired by *Emma*, one of Jane Austen's most beloved novels. (978-1-63679-879-0)

One Measure of Love by Annie McDonald. Vancouver's hit competitive cooking show *Recipe for Success* has begun filming its second season, and two talented young chefs are desperate for more than a winning dish. (978-1-63679-827-1)

The Smallest Day by J.M. Redmann. The first bullet missed—can Micky Knight stop the second bullet from finding its target? (978-1-63679-854-7)

To Please Her by Elena Abbott. A spilled coffee leads Sabrina into a world of erotic BDSM that may just land her the love of her life. (978-1-63679-849-3)

Two Weddings and a Funeral by Claudia Parr. Stella and Theo have spent the last thirteen years pretending they can be just friends, but surely "just friends" don't make out every chance they get. (978-1-63679-820-2)

Firecamp by Jaycie Morrison. Going their separate ways seemed inevitable for two people as different as Fallon and Nora, while meeting up again is strictly coincidental. (978-1-63679-753-3)

Coming Up Clutch by Anna Gram. College softball star Kelly "Razor" Mitchell hung up her cleats early, but when former crush, now coach Ashton Sharpe shows up on her doorstep seven years later, beautiful as ever, Razor hopes the longing in her gaze has nothing to do with softball. (978-1-63679-817-2)

Fixed Up by Aurora Rey. When electrician Jack Barrow and artist Ellie Lancaster get stuck on a job site during a blizzard, close quarters send all sorts of sparks flying. (978-1-63679-788-5)

Stranded by Ronica Black. Can Abigail and Whitley overcome their personal hang-ups and stubbornness to survive not only Alaska but a dangerous stalker as well? (978-1-63679-761-8)